ENEMY'S SECRET

An Enemies to Lovers Second Chance Romance

Love Comes to Town Book 2

ASHLEE PRICE

https://www.ashleepriceromanceauthor.com/

CHAPTER 1

Landon

They say time heals all wounds, but I'd say it just ripped me a new one. Over a nine-year-old scar.

Kyra Fucking Masterson.

Same inky hair, Snow White skin, same pouting red lips. Is that why I'm getting a hard-on just from a glance?

Granted, her tight little body looks hot as hell in that two-piece grey pinstripe suit, and the hard wooden surface of the stand would be perfect for bending her over and...

Not now, Landon.

But I can't peel my eyes away. Shit, everything about her looks the same, but... better somehow. Different. I can't put my finger on it.

"This is why, your honor, we are here today to discuss the plagiarism charges against Storm Media," Kyra says in that same throaty voice I had grown so used to. Although right now there's a sharp edge to it that will allow nothing but agreement. "Because there's more than enough evidence to warrant it."

My lawyer, Dirk, states some kind of defense, meant to shut this all down. With the shit-show going on around Storm Media already - we're getting audited by the IRS thanks to Dad's shady finances - the last thing we need is Goldtree Inc. getting dirt on us too. With Greyson's latest TV series, we've managed to avoid the red, but another scandal - or worse, a big payout - could put us right back there. Not that Dirk is coming cheap.

Nevertheless, as much as I hate to admit it, I'm actually slightly enjoying this. Seeing Kyra in her element. Sure, I'm focused more on the appealing way those pouty lips are moving than on the actual words coming out of them, but still.

"We will continue to examine the evidence brought before us over the coming weeks," the judge is saying now. "Court dismissed."

Outside the room, in the lobby, I call up Nolan.

"Did we win?" he asks.

"Dude, it was the first day."

"Well." He sniffs. "Maybe we got lucky. I am a lucky person, you know."

"Course I do. You got to be my brother, after all."

Nolan snorts. "Also, just an FYI, your dog shit on my rug."

"It was an ugly rug," I say blandly. "Anyway, you have to listen to this - "

"Hello? Did you not hear me? After I did you the hugely awesome, major favor of babysitting your psycho stray mutt, he goes and lets a big one loose on my sustainably-bred alpaca fur rug! Now, I don't know what could be more important than that, but - "

"I saw Kyra."

"Oh." I can almost see the smile creeping over Nolan's face. "The Kyra?"

"No, one of the many Kyras that inhabit our city. Yes, of course it was the Kyra!"

"Where'd you see her?"

"Get this: she's the lawyer for Goldtree Inc."

Nolan laughs loudly. "Well, you're done for. Remember how much she studied in school? Seemed like every time I saw her she had her nose buried in a book."

"Glad you're so optimistic about our chances," I say drily. "Anyway, book smart does not a good lawyer make."

"Hmm," Nolan says blandly.

"Alright, she's amazing in court," I say. "And hotter than ever."

"Too bad you screwed that thing up," Nolan says meditatively. "Now, I bet all the Storm charm in the world wouldn't make that right. Mind if I step in?"

I know he's just messing with me - not dating each other's exes is one of the basics of twin etiquette - but still, I snap: "I bet I could win her over if I wanted to."

"Nah." Nolan chuckles, and if he were here, he'd be shaking his head. "No way."

"I did it once," I say. "Can't be so hard to do it again. Plus, it would help get the case against Storm Media thrown out."

"Dude," Nolan says. "Last time you saw her, you - "

A tap on my shoulder. I turn around.

"Got to go," I tell Nolan, hanging up as soon as I see who it is.

There she is: dark long-lashed eyes narrowed, pretty lips curled into a sneer, arms crossed over her chest.

"Word to the wise," she says. "Don't talk about someone when they're in the same room."

God she's pretty. Plus, there's this edge about her now that's driving me wild.

"Kyra, hey." I smile. "Imagine running into you here."

She doesn't smile. "I heard you, you know."

"Huh?"

"Don't act dumb. 'I bet I could win her over if I wanted to.' God, you haven't changed one bit."

"Listen, it's not what you think - "

A sharp bark of a laugh. "Oh really? So it wasn't Nolan you were bragging to?"

I pause, deflated. "OK, so maybe - "

She heads off. "Forget it. I've got to get home."

"Kyra," I say, following her. "Just hold on - it's been good seeing you, even under the circumstances."

The look she gives me manages to be both bland and hateful at once. "Wish I could say the same." Eyeing me, she shakes her head. "God, you really think we're back in college, don't you? That I still can't resist you."

I try to smile. Since apologizing hasn't been working, maybe a bit of humor? "Well, you were crazy about me."

"Key word being were. Now?" Her chin lifts. Her eyes flash. "I hate you."

"Whoa there, hate? That's a bit much." I try to smile, but find that I can't. The way 'hate' rolled off her tongue so easily shook me.

"Not really," she says with a light eat-shit smile. "Anyway, I'll be seeing you."

"No, Kyra, just hold on a second." I move to block her path. Shit, why can't I just let her leave? "You don't really hate me." Why do I even care?

"Yeah, I really do," she says. "Think about it, Landon - there aren't many things worse than seeing your ex again." Her eyes narrow with thought, then her head tilts to the side. "OK, maybe getting a lobotomy, having your pants rip in the ass, and your dad and best friend getting married, but since I've been lucky enough not to experience those - I'm going to go."

She storms away, then pauses. "Oh, and Landon?"

"Yeah?"

"If it wasn't clear before, I still hate you. After that stunt you pulled back in college, I'd rather drink bleach than go out with you again."

God, talk about a psycho. Maybe I was a dick when I pulled that 'stunt', but still.

I find myself snapping too. "Good, because I hate you too."

Whoa - what now?

Her sculpted eyebrows arc. "Good."

"Good."

"I'm leaving now."

"Good."

"We're going to win this case and take your crooked ass down," she snaps.

"Yeah, you go and try that," I snap back.

And then she's gone and I can't seem to pry my eyes off her ass.

Where the hell did that come from? Obviously, I don't hate Kyra, even if she is being a major bitch. Then why blurt it out?

Maybe her saying she'd rather drink bleach than go out with me brought it on. Or how she kept saying 'I hate you' like it was a saw that could cut through me. Or how, despite all of this, I've got a hard-on that says she's hotter than ever.

Fuck it, I have to get home. Break the news to Greyson, then figure out what to do myself. Something tells me that Kyra and Goldtree Inc. aren't going to back down easy.

"Landon, glad I found you." It's Dirk, his face as impassive as ever.

"Haven't been hiding," I reply.

"Maybe you should." The crack of a smile that doesn't reach his eyes is the only indication that my lawyer just told a joke. "I don't want to worry you, but they have a good case. A damn good one."

"Good enough to not get thrown out of court," I say neutrally.

"Listen," he says. "Your dad has already had his name dragged through the mud this past year. Accusations of this kind aren't seeming as far-fetched as they once did."

"Accusations of this kind..." I shake my head, scowling. "My dad was a lot of things, Dirk, but he didn't copy other companies. He didn't need to."

"I know. Thing is, this Goldtree has quite the case. That doesn't mean they're going to win, though."

I eye him. "What's your point?"

"My point is that it's going to be a close one. So don't go pissing off Ms. Masterson."

"We were just talking. Why does it matter, anyway?"

"She's well-known around here. Killer at her job." Dirk's eyes narrow significantly. "And apparently even more killer when she's upset. She's credited with single-handedly revamping Ontario's hunting laws after a family member got hurt by a hunter. So don't piss her off."

I shrug. "I think that ship has sailed."

"Then don't piss her off further."

I glare at him. "Really? That's our game plan: don't piss off the opposing side's lawyer? That's what we're paying you for?"

"Careful," Dirk says quietly, rubbing his temples. "I'm doing this case partly as a favor, a thanks for all the times your father had my back. We both know The Ronald refused to touch this case with a ten-foot stick."

I grimace. It really is a measure of how low public opinion of Storm Media has sunk that even Ronald flat-out refuses to represent us - he almost represented O. J. Simpson, for Christ's sake.

"I will be careful," I say smoothly, turning to go. This conversation is long past its expiry date. "And we will win."

There's no other option. Although, as I'm leaving the building, it's not our win that's clogging my head. It's her.

Kyra.

Smiling that hateful smile.

CHAPTER 2

Kyra

"Fuck him, fuck him, fuck him," I grumble over whatever too-happy pop song is on the radio.

At the red light, I mash the station button until I get to an angry punk song that better expresses my current mood. "How fucking dare he."

It wasn't enough that he acted like the tool of the century back in college - he had to make a go of it again. I recognized the avid way he gazed at me, his easy smile, all too well. He was on the hunt. He saw something he liked.

"Well, fuck him, because it's not going to happen," I snap to myself. "Ever."

Even if my heart is skipping a beat now and I'm still jittery with adrenaline, so what? I was an idiot to fall for him the first time, and I'm not about to do it again. God, I should've figured he'd be literally the exact same jerk as before.

He wasn't a jerk until the very end... a small voice in my head reminds me.

And all at once, I'm back there - lunch dates on that grassy hill with the willow tree, the Tim Hortons blueberry muffin he'd always pick up for me before class, the intricate diagrams he painstakingly sketched out in Economics even though I was the visual learner, not him. A boat ride for my birthday, an impromptu trip to Montreal for Christmas. A promise ring for our anniversary, topping off the sweetest weekend in a cabin in the forest I could've asked for. He was Lan, I was Kyky. He kept a picture of me in his wallet. A whole corner of his closet he kept open for my things. The two of us touring Battery Park City, as if we were really buying a house in New York's most expensive neighborhood together - the look in his eyes as he looked at the nicest house there, then me, and said, "Someday..."

"Fuck it," I say.

The end is what counted, what changed everything. The end is all that matters. No use in remembering anything else.

Like how his smile is still the same: slightly pulled up on the left side. How his light brown hair is better styled now, his hazel eyes touched with an almost permanent amusement...

No. Fuck him.

I did hate him. I do. After what he did to me, I don't care how many mindfulness gurus or self-help books tell me that forgiveness is cleansing for the soul or whatever-else bullshit - I'm not going for it. Maybe rage and hate is toxic for some people, but not for me. It's what's driven me to become the woman I am. The mother I am. If I get rid of that rage, all that's left is a sad pit. And I can't afford that.

I pull up to the school, and minutes later, Madison comes out. I change the station to the third button down: the kid's classical channel I have saved.

"Hey Mom," she says, as calming Debussy trills through the car.

And just like that, the iron grip on my heart releases.

"Hey," I say. "Have fun at school?"

Madison looks at me with serious hazel eyes, like I've lost my marbles. "Always, Mom."

"That's what I like to hear," I say, pulling out and driving away.

"We made paper cranes and let the wind take them. It was so funny, Mommy."

"I'll bet. What was yours like?"

Madison bites her lip. "I used some of the Babar stickers."

"That's OK, honey. You know that's what I gave them to you for."

"I know... But now I'll never see them again. The wind took them."

"You never know - maybe the wind will bring them back." I find myself smiling vaguely. "Life has a way of surprising you."

Preach. Although, like today, not all of its surprises are good - or in any way wanted.

Why couldn't Landon have stayed in his stupid office where he belonged? It was bad enough seeing him and his brothers splashed across the papers every other month - now I have to see him every few days in court?

Back at home, we're working on some more paper cranes when the phone rings.

"How'd it go?" Pamela asks.

"Good," I say. "Judge agreed we have a case."

"Score!" I can almost see her freckled face beaming at the news. She pauses. "Why don't you sound more psyched about it?"

Ugh, just tell her.

But I don't want to. Living through it once was enough - do I really have to recap?

"You saw him, didn't you?" Pamela says quietly. "Landon."

"Yeah, well, it wasn't totally unexpected." I force a laugh. "He's president of Storm Media now. What did I expect?"

A representative, another brother, maybe... oh, who was I kidding? I've been dreading this court date for weeks.

"I better come over," Pamela says gently.

"No, no, honestly it's fine," I say. "Madison and I are just doing crafts. It's soothing, really."

"Madison goes to bed in like a half hour," Pamela says. "And then you'll get to watching Angel and sipping that horrible sad mint tea you like and... that's it. I'm coming."

"Fine," I say. "But we aren't finishing a whole pint of Ben and Jerry's mint ice cream like last time."

"Last time was nine years ago," Pamela says with a sniff. "I don't think bingeing on ice cream once every nine years is exactly grounds for a heart attack or anything."

"Alright," I say. "But we're still watching Angel."

Pamela chuckles. "I wouldn't have it any other way."

An hour or so later, after Madison's been tucked in, my doorbell rings.

"Sorry I'm a bit late," Pamela says, grocery bag on arm.

I roll my eyes. "Are we honestly trying to recreate the last time? Because it was bad enough then."

"No-o-o," Pamela says. "Just - ice cream makes everything better."

"That I can't argue with," I admit. "And you got the mint?"

"Did I get the mint," Pamela says, with her own eye roll, then sighs. "Yeah, they were actually out, so Rocky Road will have to do."

"I'm just glad you're here," I say.

She hugs me, and I hug her back, hard. "Don't worry. You're going to get through this. You already did once."

"I know," I say. "I'm not worried. It's just annoying, more than anything."

She nods. "Right. Want to talk first, or Angel?"

"Why not both?"

Pamela tosses a red curl out of her face with a smirk. "We have watched every season like - what - eight times?"

"You can never over-watch a masterpiece," I say firmly.

"Yeah, and it has nothing to do with the fact that Landon looks like Angel, at all," Pamela says significantly.

"None whatsoever," I reply icily.

A few minutes later, we're plopped on my couch in front of season three of Angel, eating Rocky Road out of the tub.

"Kyra," Pamela says quietly. "It's OK if you're not completely OK, you know."

Something I'd been holding tight loosens. "I know. It's just... I can't afford to take my eyes off the goal. But seeing him like that - and how he acted. Just like before. Just like in the beginning. You know - crazy about me. Like there's nothing else on earth he wants. Except me."

"That dick," Pamela mutters.

"But that's the thing," I say. "That's just Landon. He sees something he wants, he goes for it all-out. He isn't doing it to screw with me or anything." I scowl. "But then how he gloated to Nolan over the phone, like he was some big-shot who could get me, easy. Ugh. I just wish I could... forget it."

"Get him back for what he did to you?" Pamela wonders with an evil grin.

A smile touches my face, although I don't reply.

"Why not?" she presses. "He deserves it."

"Maybe," I say. "But I can't afford to take my eye off the goal. I just have to get through this case in one piece, hopefully even win it. Anyway, maybe this will be my revenge: seeing his company finally sunk by all the unethical things they've done."

"Hell yeah." Pamela grins. "It's my company they screwed over."

I shake my head. "It just seems so unlike him, Storm Media, even - plagiarism. Although I guess I shouldn't be surprised, with all the other sketchy shit they're embroiled in lately."

Pamela lightly squeezes my hand. "You don't really know him anymore, Ky."

"I know, Pompom." I close my eyes. "Not sure I ever did."

I force a smile as I lean my head on her shoulder. "Although I do know one thing."

"Yeah?"

"I never would've gotten through the break-up or these past years without you. Honestly."

"Hey, you would've done the same for me, if I had a relationship that lasted more than five minutes," she says with a chuckle. "And by the way: yes, you totally would've gotten through it. Now, speaking of, did I tell you about my insane date with that Italian chef?"

"No." I sit up, a smile climbing on my face. Yes, a change of subject was long overdue.

I've spent enough time being sad over Landon to last me two lifetimes.

CHAPTER 3

Landon

"If it wasn't clear before, I still hate you", her voice echoes in my head as I drive home.

My hands tighten on the steering wheel just as my cock flexes. For fuck's sake, why am I getting another hard-on just thinking about what a bitch Kyra was?

Maybe because there's something of a challenge in it. Unlike Nolan, always playing video games on the easy level, going for whatever bar slut gives him the most intense fuck-me eyes, I've always liked a challenge.

But Kyra isn't a challenge. She's suicide. I heard her - "I'd rather drink bleach than go out with you again." Then why do I get the feeling she was saying it as much to shield herself as to push me away?

It doesn't matter. Kyra is the definition of no-go zone. I was a dick to her before; the least I can do now is leave her the fuck alone. I screwed up. And no matter how much I regret it, I need to go away and stay away.

Easier said than done, now that I'll be seeing her in court every week.

Fuck, what I wouldn't do for ten minutes with her in a closed room...

Landon.

I can't go down this road, even mentally. I need to stay focused to win this case. I'm the President of Storm Media now. There's no room for mistakes. Nothing less than complete annihilation of any threat - Goldtree's case included.

My phone goes off, but I don't answer it. Most likely it's Nolan, wanting to know why I hung up on him. He maybe has some event or two he wants us to hit up. It never gets old for him, us being twins. It's an easy ice-breaker with girls, a cute conversation piece with clients and new acquaintances. A few times a year, he'll even cut his hair like mine so that we can switch places, just to mess with people.

OK, it can be a bit funny, and a bit of comic relief would help take my mind off it. How the two sides of Kyra's dark, sleek hair are like two arrows pointing straight to her breasts. Or how she carries herself differently. Is she really as different as it seems, or is this all part of her I'm-a-lawyer-don't-fuck-with-me persona?

I pull into my building's underground parking lot with a shake of my head. It doesn't matter. I'll only be seeing her in a professional capacity.

But as the elevator whizzes up to my penthouse suite, she won't get out of my head. In the mirror, I see that pretty face crumple with my cock inside her. That angry sneer slacken as she moans my name.

Ding

I scowl, hurrying out of the elevator and into my apartment.

Fuck. So much for getting Kyra out of my head. Looks like I'll have to get her out of my system entirely.

I roll my eyes when I realize that I'm seriously considering Nolan's 'theory', if you can even call it that. He's convinced it works, though.

Whenever he has a major crush on a girl or just can't get her out of his head, he jerks off to her. Apparently, that's enough to do it for him - clear his mind, 'free' him, whatever. He still finds her hot, obviously, but he 'gets it out of his system'. Or so he claims.

Usually, I'm able to get a girl out of my system by actually fucking her, but considering the circumstances... this will have to do.

In the shower, I turn the shower head on high so that the hot droplets splatter my body, easing my tired muscles. That's another thing that could help clear my mind - the gym, the wall. Not now, though. I need her gone - now.

But before that, I need to be inside her.

I can see it now: the judge gone, everyone else gone - just the two of us. The two of us and an empty courtroom, and everything I want to do to her.

She'd try to say it again, "I hate you," but I'd beat her to it. My kiss would slam the words right out of her mouth, my tongue would lap the thought right out of her head.

Her body would give in how it wanted to.

Maybe at first, she'd rip away, still glaring, opening her mouth to snap something else.

Another kiss would shut up those pretty lips.

I'd cup each breast and enjoy them through her tight work shirt. She'd groan.

And now I have her in my arms, carrying her over to the podium. Pressing her into it, our lips twisting together. Fuck it's good. So fucking good.

Her skin is just as silky as I remember. Her lips move on mine with abandon, following my lead. She tastes like victory and strawberries. Fuck yeah.

Her work shirt undoes easily and underneath is a black dominatrix style X-bra. Our eyes meet. Hers are mocking, still sneering.

"Fuck you," she says.

I slam my lips to hers again, press myself into her. Pulling away, enjoying the want battling the hate on her face, I say, "Fuck you."

And then we do.

Lips re-meet, fingers rip at each other, shedding the layers between us. Her skin is creamy, pale, soft, glorious. It's all so fast and hot that I hardly notice until my cock slips inside her.

Everything slackens. Fucking. Yeah. Just there. Just now.

She's wet and responsive as fuck and clasping on me. I don't even need to move, it's so good. It. This. Us. Her. Yeah.

Fucking Kyra Masterson.

And then, suddenly, I can't take it anymore. Just being inside of her isn't enough for me.

I slam into her again, enjoying how her face crumples. Another slam, and she groans.

I grunt. It feels fucking amazing.

In and out. Deep and deeper. More. More. More.

My arms around her, I kiss her hard and good.

I turn her around, press her into the podium, ram her so good and hard it starts shaking. Her groans echo through the room.

"That's it," I growl.

Half-gasping, she snarls, "I still hate you, you know."

I laugh. "Good."

And then I ram her for all I'm worth. Let her hate me. I'll still have her screaming my name by the time this is over.

"Yes, yes!" she's groaning, shaking all over.

"I want to hear it," I rasp into her ear as I drill her. "Say my name."

"Fuck you," she groans.

I pause. Her pussy clasps onto my cock desperately.

She groans. "Landon!"

"That's it." I start up again, and her moaning gets louder. "What's that, baby?"

"Landon!" she shrills, as she comes.

I don't stop now, though. I ride out her orgasm, fucking her so hard that she sinks down and I have to hold her upright with my arms. Fuck is it hot. When I feel her shaking again with another orgasm, I let loose, spilling into her.

She's still wet. It's wet everywhere. I'm -

My eyes snap open.

In the shower. Right.

As pleasure spills out of me, I frown. That little fantasy went on for far longer than normal or even necessary. Normally, a few minutes with a good porno and I'm all set. Why the fucking novel about fucking Kyra?

I wash myself off, turn off the shower, then step out. It doesn't matter, at any rate. It's done. My head is clear. I'm free of her.

I've barely sat down to eat when my intercom buzzes.

"Helloooo, rooooom serrrrrvice," a put-on nasally voice I still recognize says.

"Fuck off, Nolan," I say, hanging up. I press the button to let him in.

When he comes up, though, I see that he's not alone.

"Were there plans I missed?" I ask my brothers.

"Not exactly," Greyson says. He looks about as happy to be here as I'm feeling. "Just thought a little brother talk was in order."

"At CANOE," Emerson chimes in. "Drinks on me?"

That's our baby brother, always trying to play peacekeeper.

"Come onnn," Nolan whines when I don't respond. "We haven't had one of these in weeks. Besides, shit is hitting the fan."

Always one for the eloquently upbeat quips, my twin.

"Fine," I agree. "But we aren't staying up half the night like last time."

"We didn't stay up half the night," Nolan argues. "We were in bed at like, 4:00 AM."

I roll my eyes. "You're right - that's closer to all night."

"Besides, Greyson's a dad now," Emerson chimes in.

Greyson rubs his eyes. "Don't remind me. We just got Dakota used to a decent sleep schedule last week and I'm praying that he actually sticks to it."

"Don't pretend you don't love it." Nolan makes a face. "I mean, if it were me it really would be a living hell, this whole one woman and baby thing. But I saw you on your wedding day."

"Fuck off." Greyson scowls, but I can see he's trying not to smile.

Yep, he's crazy about that woman and kid. Anyone with eyes can see it.

"Enough wife and baby talk," I cut in. "We going out or not?"

"We're going." Nolan's already heading to the door. "Emerson had me at 'drinks on me'."

At CANOE, Emerson orders us all fancy cocktails, then Greyson folds his hands on the table. "So. These plagiarism claims. What's the deal?"

I quirk an eyebrow at him.

"Right," he says, with an apologetic smile. "Sorry. Old habits die hard."

After all, Greyson was the President before me. The role went to him after our dad died unexpectedly. But Greyson didn't enjoy it, and he stepped down several months ago to be the producer on our new Storm Media TV series, giving the title to me. He's helped me and coached me along the way, but we still aren't totally settled into our new roles. Plus, he is still the eldest.

"Forget it," I say. "We do need to talk about it."

"Don't tell me," Nolan says gloomily, already downing the last of his drink. "Another shitacular legacy of Colin Storm."

While our dad was a business and media superpower when he was alive, he was also, as we've learned since his death, an asshole. The kind of asshole who not only left the company's books in an illegal mess, but secretly diverted company funds to the Costa Rican government for priority access to film the new streaming series as well. Not to mention these plagiarism claims we're dealing with now.

"Nothing conclusive has been found yet," I say. "But what has been found suggests that the premise for the Storm TV nature series was plagiarized from Goldtree Inc."

"But is it true?" Emerson asks.

I shrug, leaning back in the booth. "Don't know. Dirk hasn't found anything. Wouldn't put it past Dad, though."

"So, what do we do?" Greyson asks, forehead creased. He has as much to lose from this case as any of us. He and Harley have killed themselves making Storm TV a success, and it's still their passion project.

Nolan leans over to give me a light punch. "Landon here left out the best part."

I glare at him. "Best part?"

He shrugs, giving his long light brown hair a derisive shake. "Alright - our best chance." He turns to the others. "Guess who the lawyer for Goldtree is?"

They give him blank stares.

"Uh... The Ronald, since he left us high and dry, and won't return our calls, and is rumored to have actually left Florida for the first time in months?" Emerson quips after a minute.

We chuckle.

"Close, but no," Nolan says. "Remember little Kyra Masterson?"

Greyson's jaw drops. "No."

"Yes," I say. "Unfortunately. I can't see why Nolan thinks this is a good thing."

Nolan's glare flicks to me, outraged. "You told me yourself that you could win her over if you wanted to."

"That was before she overhead me telling you that, then told me she hated me and that she'd rather drink bleach than go out with me again."

"Drink bleach." Emerson winces. "Ooh."

"Ooh is right," I say. "So yeah, that's not happening."

"We should just try to win the case fair and square," Greyson says. "We aren't like Dad."

Nolan takes his drink and downs it. "Nothing wrong with using every advantage available to us. Although in this case, yeah, looks like there's a grand total of none."

I roll my eyes. "Thanks for the vote of confidence." My glance goes to the others. "Anyone else have any ideas?"

"Yeah." Nolan's all smiles. "Don't piss off Kyra. Pray and beg for mercy."

"Too late," I say. "Seriously, after overhearing our conversation, she verbally ripped me a new one. If she didn't hate me before, she most definitely does now."

"Well, at least she's hot," Nolan says blandly.

Greyson snorts. "Thank God for that. We may lose the case, and even our main source of profit right now, but at least the lawyer responsible for it is hot."

Already, her face is creeping into my mind, mad and hot, with those arched eyebrows curved into a V, lips red pouting and ready and -

"Hello? Earth to twin?" Nolan intones.

I come to, to find a waitress waiting, all eyes on me.

"Sorry," I say. "What's up?"

"Emerson is buying us pity drinks," Nolan says. "Want one?"

"Sure," I say.

At this point, the only thing we really can do is drink and hope for the best.

Although once the drinks come and I sip mine, I get another brain wave. "Why don't we look into it ourselves?"

"Isn't that what the lawyers are for?" Emerson asks, sipping at his.

"Yes, except we can't afford to pay them 24/7," I explain. "We need to be saving as much money as we can, especially with the profits of our new TV series on the line. If we look into it ourselves, however..."

"Dibs on not doing it," Nolan says.

I glare at him while he assumes an unconvincing innocent expression. "What? You know how I am with research. I pass out, fall asleep, die a premature death."

"I can help," Greyson says. "Although I'll have to check with Harley as to when. She's been with Dakota almost 24/7 lately - she's more than overdue for a little break."

"I can too," Emerson says, trying to smile reassuringly but only succeeding in looking less-than-eager. "But where do we start?"

"We start with looking at the claim Goldtree submitted," I say. "And looking into the company itself. See if Dad met with them at any point, had any connections who worked there, etc. I mean, if he plagiarized from them, then he had to have met or talked with someone who worked there at some point."

Greyson nods, eyeing his drink thoughtfully. "True." He rises. "I'm going to compile a list of Goldtree's top employees, or at least the ones involved in their broadcasting division."

I rise. "I appreciate your involvement, but don't you think I should be doing that?"

"No," he says. "You have more important things to be focusing on."

As soon as he says it, I realize I've missed the obvious. "Right - Dad's close friends and business associates. I'll have Madeline compile a list of them and call them up myself. They could've heard something about this Goldtree TV show if it was a big enough deal, or even know something more specific."

"Will they really jump at admitting anything that could implicate Dad in plagiarism?" Nolan wonders aloud.

"Not the way I'll put it," I say. "We can decide what to do with the information once we have it, but I'll promise them we're going to protect Dad at all costs."

"You mean you're going to lie," Nolan says helpfully.

"No." I sit back down. "I mean that I'm going to do what I have to do. Keeping Storm Media out of trouble might mean protecting Dad, unfortunately. We need to know the truth if we're going to figure out what to do with it.

"At any rate, it's a start," I add.

Nolan lifts his glass. "Well, I'll drink to that."

CHAPTER 4

Kyra

God, I love winning.

The feeling when you're at the precipice of a big case, one second away from everything being worth it. I even love the times like now, when you can feel yourself inching towards that moment inexorably, unavoidably.

"That's all for today," I say, smiling wide at the rheumy-eyed judge, then at Landon, who looks pissed enough to storm out on the spot. "The evidence speaks for itself."

The judge rubs at the white tuft on his chin contemplatively. "It would appear so. Court dismissed for today."

As I stride out, Landon calls after me, "Hey, wait!"

"Sorry," I say. "Not in the mood for another yesterday."

"Guess I'll keep your case binder, then," he says easily.

I pause. Sure enough, the jerk has my binder in his hands, is holding it out for me.

I take it, then continue walking off.

"Would a 'thanks' kill you?" he asks.

Don't stop - don't stop - don't -

I turn around to glare at him. "You're right, I should be falling all over myself for you showing basic human decency. After all, it probably is a stretch for you."

A smile plays on his face. "You're really determined to hate me, aren't you?"

I shoot him a sweet smile. "Doesn't take much determination."

He cocks his head to one side, smiles that stupid one-sided smile. "Oh yeah?"

I turn around again. "Yeah. Now, if you'll excuse me - "

"I'm sorry, you know."

I pause. My back stiffens. Here it is. What I'd been aching to hear for years - years - now, too many years too late.

"Kyra, did you hear me?"

I exhale. "Are you being serious right now?"

Despite my better instincts not to waste another second here, not to give the tool so much as a second look, I glance his way.

"What?" he says.

Stay cool. Just let him say whatever it is he needs to say, then leave. "What are you sorry for?"

"For yesterday, for what happened back in college. I'm sorry, Kyra."

I nod. "OK."

He adjusts his stance. "OK..."

My glare cuts to him. "What - am I supposed to be jumping up and down ecstatically?"

"No. I just... thought I should get that out of the way."

I nod. "Well. Right. OK. Now that you've gotten that out of the way, can I leave?"

He stands there, gaping at me. As if he expected a fricking Nobel Peace Prize or something.

"Am I supposed to be impressed that you're apologizing now of all times? Years too late? After you proved that you're exactly the same jerk as before?"

"No," he says. "I mean... I didn't even say it to intend anything. It just came out."

I stare into his eyes. Yes, Landon, I know you when you see something you want - you'll do anything, absolutely anything, to get it. And I won't be won over by a cheap apology made way too late. No way.

"Can we just start over?" he's asking now.

"No," I say. "We can't. Now, I have to go. I would wish you luck, except I like to win and I'm going to beat you. And best of all, I'm going to enjoy it."

As I turn on my heel and walk away, I can't help a self-satisfied smile taking over my face.

"I wouldn't count on it," he growls after me. "Just remember, Kyra: I always get what I want."

I'm glad I'm practically out of the room, so he can't see the shiver that goes through me.

**

The rest of the day goes as usual: I pick up Madison from school, we cook something fun together (tonight it's feta-filled ravioli with homemade basil pasta sauce), I tuck her into bed and read The Travels of Babar to her. Then it's lights-out and I have some much-needed me time. Sinking onto the couch, I've just put on some New Girl season four when my phone rings.

"Hello?" I say.

I don't normally pick up for unknown numbers, but with this case going on, new information could come from any and everywhere.

"Hey," a horribly familiar voice says.

Shit.

I'd know that voice anywhere. And just like that, I'm very, very mad.

"Seriously?" I snap. "Who gave you this number?"

"Maybe I'm prepared to make a deal."

"Don't bullshit me. Now, I'm hanging up."

"Don't - just wait, Kyky."

"Don't call me that."

My finger's poised, about to hang up. But I can't quite make myself. Not yet.

"I want to make it up to you. Call a truce."

"I don't want that."

"Unfortunate," he says.

"Yeah, for you. Now, I just started a show - "

"You realize I'm not going to stop, don't you?"

"So you're stalking me now? Cute. Lucky for me, there's this thing called a restraining order that works nicely for cases like yours."

"Just let me take you out. One dinner."

"Why?"

"To make it up to you?"

"To schmooze your way into a better case outcome, you mean."

And maybe even into my pants, I add inwardly.

"To settle it. If after the dinner you want me to leave you alone for good, I will."

"And let me guess. If I don't agree, you'll keep bothering me."

I can hear the smile in his voice. "Something like that. Yeah."

"So, blackmail?"

"You get a free meal out of it, so what's the problem?"

"The problem is the company."

"Ky - "

"No," I say suddenly. "I don't care what you do. I won't."

I hang up before he can answer.

I sink into the couch, breathing deep. That was close. Too close.

In a fast, furious autopilot, I snap off the TV, take off my makeup, brush my teeth. Floss. Put on my night cream, then throw myself into bed.

Screw today. Screw Landon. Screw whatever thought I almost had. Whatever stupid crap I almost considered.

The only thing that can fix today is tomorrow. Sleep.

**

Weird. I went to sleep to escape him, but now here's here.

He climbs into bed with me, covers me with his arms. "Don't pretend you don't want this."

His mouth eats my protest, his hands stroke away my tension. I groan down his throat. Kissing him is like coming home. Like eating my favorite dessert. Like picking off a scab that was never supposed to be touched.

It's freeing. Perfect.

His tongue entwines with mine, leads it how he wants to. Our hands explore each other's bodies. His is more muscular, more tense and with harder edges. He touches me with an ease and familiarity, as if it was only yesterday we did this. He knows how to touch me right and he takes full advantage of this knowledge. He strokes and massages my ass until I'm crooning.

He touches me with a quick-flitting eagerness, with an excitement like it's the very first time.

I guess in a way it is.

He strokes and kisses off my clothes, then clasps me to him tight. As if he never wants to let me go. I can feel the hardness of his cock pressing into me through his pants.

Every breath we take is like sand falling out of an hourglass towards what's inevitable.

All at once, at the same time, neither of us can take it anymore. He rips off my clothes, I rip off his. Our lips feast on each other's bodies. A gasp falls out of my mouth as his lips land on my breast.

"Yes, oh yes."

He laps at it, and pleasure sizzles in me. His hand palms my other breast. Already, I'm crazy wet.

As if hearing my thought, his hand strokes down, stopping there. His fingers sweep inside of me, and another gasp falls out.

"So wet," he growls with pleasure.

He fingers me fast and merciless, and next thing I know, I'm curled into a ball, groans that don't sound like mine dribbling out of me. I come once, then again. He doesn't so much as slow.

He pats my ass. "I still love seeing you come."

Then he clambers on top of me and plunges inside me.

Ohhhhhhhh... yes. Ohhhhhhhh... yes. Ohhhhhhhh... yes, yes.

He's massive inside me, stretching me slightly as he slowly moves in and then out again.

"As perfect as I remember," he groans.

"Please," is all I can say.

His eyes snap open, full of want. He grins. "Hell yeah."

And then he fucks me hard and good. Our bodies slap together, can't get enough. I can't. Already I'm at the edge, swollen with pleasure, crying out with it. More and more and more.

And then I'm coming, and he's spanking me, and I'm coming harder, and he's plunging inside me deeper than ever and then we're both coming.

It's glorious and perfect, until I peek open my eyes.

He's not there, of course. I'm in my bed, alone. It was only a dream.

My eyes snap open the rest of the way. "Fuck's sake, Kyra."

I scramble out of bed, straight for the shower. I can't fucking believe this. I thought I was past this. I was supposed to be past this.

I can't even bear to glance at myself as I hurry past the mirror. Instead, in the shower, I crank it up on high, and let the tears fall down and the hot water batter me. But I don't let the thoughts come, the ones at the edge of my consciousness: You screwed up. You promised this would never happen again. You're slipping.

Instead, I keep the ones I want, the only ones I can afford to have: I can do this. I can handle this. I won't make the same mistakes again.

CHAPTER 5

Landon

Fuck me.

I glare at my miserable reflection in the bathroom. Having to leave the trial for a 'bathroom break', really? When I actually came in here to jerk off.

Fuck, what am I, 13?

So what if Kyra is hot as hell, and has, coincidently, chosen today to wear a tight red suit that belongs more in an office porno than in an actual courtroom? So fucking what? If she's trying to wind me up, to keep me unbalanced, it's working. But I still won't take the bait. I won't lose my cool in court or on the stand.

I twist on the tap, shove my hands under the cool stream and splash water on my face. There. I just need another minute in here to calm down and then...

Then what?

The past few days of grilling Dad's former colleagues and getting Madeline on the hunt haven't produced much. Goldtree won't divulge their secret source, and I can't find a link from them to my dad. But there must be one - otherwise there wouldn't be a case.

Up until now Goldtree's case has been based on the similarities between our new TV show and their planned one, as well as a supposed conversation this source had with my dad months before our TV show was thought up. They even have a recording with Dad's voice, but the conversation is so vague, them talking about a 'nature documentary', that that can't be all they've got. After all, so what -

BBC Earth is a nature documentary, there's all the National Geographic wildlife and plant specials, and they aren't accusing us of plagiarizing them. Goldtree Inc. has a bombshell - I can feel it - but I need to know what it is so we can have enough time to defend ourselves against it. Fuck.

And Kyra, in her fuck-me red suit and pitiless smile... drilling away at Storm Media. She even dug up a case of Dad back in his university years plagiarizing some history paper. Jesus fucking Christ. Dad was 19, for fuck's sake.

As I leave the bathroom, Kyra's leaving the courtroom.

"Too bad you missed it." She pouts, although her eyes are dancing. "The judge wants to see all your dad's notebooks from the past five years. Thinks there might be something in them."

I eye her coolly. "Of course, he's welcome to them. We'll hand them over as soon as we have them."

"Who knows, they might actually help your case," she returns easily. "God knows you need it."

That's not all I need right now...

She rips her gaze off mine, frowning. "Oh, and Landon?"

"What?"

"Don't call me again. It's not going to win you any brownie points."

"Not doing it for that."

Her gaze snaps to mine, then retreats. "Whatever. Just leave me alone."

"My pleasure."

"Great."

"Great."

I storm out of the building, not even waiting for Dirk. I don't need to see his dire face to know that things are progressing quickly and shittily.

On the way out, I pause to try calling up Greyson. Maybe he knows where Dad's notebooks are. Kyra strides by me without a second look, then gets in her older-looking Volkswagen.

My first call to Greyson goes straight to voicemail. Next one, same thing.

Kyra rushes out of her car, phone to her ear, looking distraught.

"Hey?" I say, as she passes by.

"Don't." She waves me away, then continues talking into the phone. "Hello? Yes, I need a tow truck here immediately. I'm at the Bererier Courthouse on Blythe." A pause, presumably while they answer. "Wait, what?!?"

Her eyes bug out of her head. "You won't be able to get one here for another three hours? This is New York, for Christ's sake!"

She hangs up, muttering, "Shit, shit, shit."

"Somewhere you need to be?" I ask.

"Just - go away." She exhales hard. "I don't need this right now."

"No, what you need is a car, by the sound of it."

She hardly hears, by the looks of it, is muttering to herself, "Yeah, Mom, great freaking idea - use Dad's old Volkswagen. 'If it ain't broke, don't fix it' - except yes, it is broke and it keeps breaking and now, at the worst time possible, it's broken again!"

She forces out an exhale, gives her head a shake as though to physically dislodge the panic written all over her face. "Screw it. I'll just call a goddamn cab." She winces, probably thinking the same thing I am: cabs in New York are notoriously shit, sometimes come half an hour late - if they decide to come at all. "Or an Uber..." Jamming at her phone, she groans. "No, no... not now."

"Phone die?" I ask.

"What, come to laugh at my shitty luck?" she snarls, glaring at me.

"Nope." I shrug. "Offer for a ride is still up for grabs."

"I don't need a ride, I need a car and..." She pauses and I can almost see the gears turning in her head. "Actually, you know what? A ride would be awesome. If you could just drop me off at Pamela's place, that would be great."

"Sure," I say smoothly. "And our dinner?"

Her fists ball. "Are you actually trying to blackmail me right now? Because I'm so not in the mood."

"Wouldn't dream of it. So, are we on?"

She glares at me. "You're seriously doing this?"

I just smile, and she exhales. "Of course you're seriously doing this." She throws up her hands. "You know what? Fine. OK. Let's get this shit over with. Dinner tonight - at eight?"

"Bit late for dinner," I comment.

Her eyes narrow even further. "Tonight or never - up to you." A significant smile plays on her lips, and I have to resist the urge to tap the tip of her nose like I used to when she was being sassy. "Of course, if it were up to me, it would be never. But it seems like you've left me no choice."

"Alright, tonight it is," I say, heading for my car. "You're still friends with Pamela?"

"Well, she's never let me down," she says with a pointed look my way, following alongside.

Yep, if knife-throwing were a sport, something tells me Kyra would be a master at it.

"Can we have one normal conversation where you aren't biting my head off?" I ask.

As she gets into my car, Kyra tilts her head, pretending to think it over. "Hmm... let me see... no?"

"You know, you weren't totally in the clear back then, either," I point out, getting in myself.

"Hold on." She barks out a laugh. "Are you actually trying to excuse what you did?"

"No, not at all. It was a dick move. I just..." I shake my head. "Forget it. You knew I wasn't comfortable with your friend Andy, and you just tried to laugh it all off."

"Drop my best friend of 10 years for just happening to be a boy?" Kyra sneers. "Jealous much?"

I shrug as I start up the car. "Yeah, guess I was. What ever happened to him, anyway?"

"Can we just get to Pamela's as fast as possible, please?" Kyra's turned so she's looking out the window. "If it isn't obvious yet, I have somewhere I need to be. ASAP."

"Doctor's appointment?" I say lightly.

"Exactly," she says shortly.

Silence. She's close enough to grab, to kiss. Even her profile is hot to me. Fuck. Maybe I just need to get laid with someone new. This is beyond fucked.

I can hardly concentrate on the road, with her just a seat away. She'd look better in my lap. On my cock.

Landon.

"Pamela still lives in the same place?" I ask.

"Yep." Kyra chuckles. "The yellow paint in her bathroom's a bit more ragged, and that crazy hippy next door had her two Australian sisters move in, but that's about it."

I find myself smiling, remembering the time we played a game of drunk Uno with them. I'd never been much of a card game person, but something about that night, about how delighted Kyra was every time she got to roar "UNO!" won me over. "Some things never change."

"No, they don't," Kyra says softly, almost sadly.

We're nearly there when she speaks again, "He made a move on me."

"What?"

"Andy. Once I was single, one night we were at a bar with friends, then outside just us and - he tried kissing me."

"And?"

"And he got angry when I turned him down. Claimed I'd been leading him on for years. Our friendship kind of petered out after that."

"Well." Part of me wants to fling it in her face - 'Ha, called it! And all those times you played innocent' - but I really just like that she isn't snapping at me for once. That I'm not the one in the wrong. Except, in a way, ever since that night, I'll always be in the wrong and we both know it. "I won't pretend that I'm sorry."

"He wasn't that bad, you know," Kyra argues, face firming up now. "We just got our wires crossed along the way, and then..." She shakes her head. "It doesn't matter, anyway. People grow apart. Nearly all my old friends have."

Another forced exhale. "Don't know why I'm telling you this. Anyway - we're here."

I'd hardly noticed that I'd pulled into Pamela's weed-crowded cobblestone driveway. Maybe because I've been trying to concentrate on not kissing Kyra.

You could, now.

"Thanks," she says, opening the door. "See you tonight."

And then she's gone and the opportunity too. Good thing, probably. She's agreed to the dinner - no point in pushing things.

Although, as I drive home, I can't help but wonder what she's doing now. If it really was a doctor's appointment and, if not, why she lied about it.

CHAPTER 6

Kyra

"Kyra, hey!" Pamela's coral lips peel into a wide but surprised smile as she opens the door. "What are you doing here? Don't you have to pick up - "

"Madison, yeah," I say. "Long story short: my car broke down, I didn't trust a taxi to get me there, and my phone died too. A peach of a day, but is there any way you could give me a ride?"

"Of course!" She's already grabbing her car keys from the purple cat hook by the door and heading out. "Let's do this. What a day."

"I know," I say, following her to her blue Beetle. "But the good news is that I killed it in court today. How was your day?"

"Of course." She rolls her eyes as if it were a given as we get inside. "And you know me: same old, same old. Did the work thing, then some old man tried to argue with me about wallpaper. I put him in his place."

"You busy bee," I say. "You had time to do that and plan out Goldtree's newest cinematic offering?"

Interior decorating is her side hustle, although it's actually her passion too. It just doesn't make quite enough to pay the bills yet.

She makes a skeptical noise as she starts up the car and hits the radio - the station's playing 'Come Together', the Beatles singing away. "Honestly, there isn't much to do at work lately. I think my boss is a little too invested in this case against Storm Media, if you know what I mean."

"Jeanine has been sitting at the back for every court date," I confirm with a small smile.

She snorts. "Typical Jeanine." She honks at a pigeon slowly wobbling across the street then, as it flutters away, puts her foot on the gas. "Anyway. How is the whole Landon thing?"

"It's not a thing," I say.

"OK... how is the whole 'having to see your shitty ex at work' thing?"

"Pretty much shitty," I say.

If anyone knew how broken up and destroyed I was after the break-up, it was Pompom. She bought me an X-Large packet of 3-ply Kleenex from Costco, forged a doctor's note so I could miss an ill-timed legal exam, even helped me in a Burn-My-Ex's-Shit bonfire on a small scraggly beach. Plus, she was there when it all went down.

The smartest thing would probably be just to fess up about this whole ride and dinner thing, but I don't want to.

I don't want to see my own disappointment in myself on her face. If I'm screwing up, saying more than a single civil word to Landon, I want to be damn sure that I'm the only one who knows about it.

"How did you get to my place, though, if your phone died and your car broke down?" she wonders.

"Had to get a ride from Landon," I grumble.

"Ooh."

"Yeah. Let's not talk about it."

"He get older and fatter?"

"Nope."

"Well, he can't have gotten as much hotter as you did."

"Pompom. I really don't want to talk about it now. OK?"

"OK, OK. Forget I said anything."

"Gladly."

"After all," she continues blithely, "just another month or so of this case, and then - "

"I said I didn't want to talk about it."

"Whoa." She makes a face. "Fine, then."

"Good."

The rest of the day is on a stressful autopilot: Madison is delighted to see me, even if I am 10 minutes late to pick her up. I call a tow truck to get my car, then arrange for the mechanic to take a look at it as soon as it arrives. I thank Pompom profusely, promise her a payback dinner which she refuses, then go home and tuck Madison into bed.

"This is exciting," Mom says, jiggling her pencil-thin reddish-brown eyebrows, after she arrives a few minutes later. "You haven't been on a date in some time."

"Mom." I glare at her. "I told you, it's not a date."

"Alright then." She pouts. "A meet-up in the late hours with a like-minded acquaintance."

"Sure."

Already, I'm wondering if I should've just bitten the bullet and asked Pamela. Although I'm not exactly dying to be subjected to a Landon-is-a-jerk rant. Even if it's true.

"And as for the identity of this like-minded acquaintance..."

"I told you Mom, you don't know them."

Yes, an outright lie, but not completely. I'm not sure I even know Landon now, after all this time. Anyway, I just need to get through tonight, then I can handle seeing him every few days at the courthouse. Then everything will be like it was before. Landon will be out of my life for good. Thank God.

For some reason choosing my dress takes longer than I'd like - everything either screams 'I'm a slut' or 'I'm a nun' - and I redo my volumizing mascara three different times. I finally end up in a button-up dress that's tight, but not too tight, and forest green. Wasn't that Landon's least favorite color back in the day?

It occurs to me, as I apply a completely different red over my previously pink lipstick, that I'm trying to guarantee the success of tonight with my apparel choices. I'm trying to express 'I don't really care about tonight but I'm being polite and I normally look this good' when in reality, more times than I'd like to admit, when I have a big case going and Madison is being difficult, I get so exhausted that I wear an actual Snuggie around the house.

Eight o'clock comes both faster and slower than I expected, and before I know it, I'm climbing into Landon's Acura.

His gaze lingers on me. "Am I allowed to say you look good?"

"No." I'm careful not to look at him too long, not to let my heart skip more than one beat. I guess he won't be griping about my dress color. Too bad. "Let's just get this over with."

He chuckles. "A ringing endorsement of tonight if I've ever heard one."

"You did basically blackmail me into coming."

"And then I saved the day. So, we even now?"

"No. Not even close." We never will be.

"You manage to get to your thing on time?" he asks.

It's getting more and more awkward, not bringing up Madison. But I don't want him knowing anything more about my personal life than necessary. Anyway, if he did... he can't. I can't have him knowing. End of.

"Yeah," I say instead. "Thanks. I really... appreciated your help."

"I'm happy to. Least I can do."

I swallow. Just a few more hours, then a few more weeks. Then this will be over. Done. Finished.

God, why is his gaze tracing me like admiring fingertips? And why does it feel so goddamn good?

I keep my gaze on the scenery outside - the big box stores, the outskirts of subdivisions. Just a few more hours. That's it.

"Here," he says at some point.

I release a breath I didn't even realize I was holding.

"This is it?" I say, my head craning back.

This isn't really where I think it is... is it?

"Yeah." His smile is offhand as he opens the door. On top of this Art Deco high-rise is Balsac's - the most expensive eatery in town. Holy hell. "Always told you I'd take you here one day, didn't I?"

I freeze. He did not just go there.

When he comes over to open my car door, I don't move. "What the heck do you think you're doing?"

He winces. "OK. Sorry. Maybe that was out of line."

"Maybe?"

He scowls. "OK. It was." His gaze meets mine as it goes apologetic. "I know I messed up. Keep messing up, really. Can we just go up there and have some good food?"

The hard grit in my belly softens. Obviously, I still have to be careful, but the old Landon was never much for apologies. This one might be different. A bit.

Not different enough for me to actually consider as anything other than my opponent in court, but still. I could enjoy a meal with him tonight. I could do that.

"Fine," I say. "Just no more bringing up the past."

His hand flies to his heart. "Soldier's honor."

I chuckle. "The only soldier you've been is in Call of Duty."

Landon grins. "Guilty as charged. Now - you ready?"

"Ready as I'll ever be," I say, going out.

As we walk towards the entrance, Landon holds out an arm.

"Seriously?" I say.

He pauses, and his arm wilts. "You really do hate me, don't you?"

There's something about the way he says it, the sad certainty replacing the cocksure persona, that gets me.

I look away. "Hate is a strong word."

"It's the one you used."

"Let's just say dislike and leave it at that."

Landon winces, exhales. "You know - if you really want to go..."

"Really?"

Again, not like the Landon I used to know, getting what he wanted, no matter the cost.

"I mean, I'd rather you stay, but if you're just going to suffer the whole time..."

"I'm not going to suffer," I say, striding by him for the door. "The food here is supposed to be amazing, after all. Plus, I've never been."

Behind me, he barks out a laugh. "Right. Great."

I feel like laughing myself - though it would be a half-hysterical one. What the hell am I doing?

Landon just gave me the perfect out - why not take it?

But the surprised happiness in his eyes is so genuine and the way he's looking at me is so intent that I can't go back on what I said now.

Landon opens the glass door for me and gestures me in. "After you."

That was one thing about Landon: he always was a gentleman. Until he wasn't.

Inside, we take a quiet, brass-applique elevator to the top, then go to the maitre d', who already has a reservation under Landon's name.

Landon has to tug me along, I'm so overawed by our surroundings. There's a reason this is the most expensive eatery in New York and it's not just the damn good food.

This place is gorgeous. We walk over brocade-embossed black and silver flooring while juxtaposed long overhangs of light illuminate our way. The walls are creamy marble, the chairs embossed teal leather. I'm practically drooling when we take our seats.

It's obviously the best table in the house, right beside the rose-tinted window, higher than every other table in the place. If this place has rulers, we're sitting at their table and sipping their water.

"Hi," Landon says.

It's only now, with Landon across from me, that I'm struck by how inconveniently handsome he is. He's in a purple shirt, with the lightest of scruff. His light brown hair has the tousled look it always gets. And those pale blue eyes have that odd light in them they used to get whenever he looked at me.

"Hi," I say.

"What's new?"

"Oh, nothing much. You?"

"Same." He scowls, then shakes his head. "OK, let's cut the shit. A lot has happened. My dad died. My brother stepped down and made me President. I'm still figuring that out."

"I'm sorry," I say. "Your dad was always a great guy."

"Great guy, yes." Landon nods. "Ethical guy?" He gulps the rest of his water, frowning. "Jury still out on that one."

"Wait." Did he just admit what I think he did? "Are you saying..."

"God, no." He frowns. "You really want to talk about the plagiarism charges here?"

"No, obviously not." I frown right back at him. "You were the one who brought it up."

"Let's just forget it," he says.

"Agreed."

His gaze slants my way. "And you?"

Here it is: the question I've been dreading. The question I have to avoid. Again. At all costs.

"Well, clearly I got through school, so that was a relief. And now, yeah, life is good. I'm a lawyer. Pamela's still my best friend."

...And I have a nine-year-old.

Landon's gaze on me is admiring, although it seems miles away too, as if trying to figure out a calculus problem. "You just seem so... different."

"People do change in nine years. Isn't that the whole point you've been trying to make about yourself?"

"Yes - and no." He smiles helplessly. "I'm still as into you as I ever was."

Fuck me. Why is it the more he says things that he shouldn't, the more excited I get?

But then it hits me, as hot and angry and certain as a fire ant: Guys who are actually into their girlfriends don't break up with them - and certainly not like that.

"Sorry," he says quickly, before I can say anything more. "You still into Kate Morton?"

"She keeps writing books, so of course. I'm surprised you remembered."

"Yeah, I had this whole meet and greet mapped out..."

"Stop it," I say quietly. "Just stop. This doesn't make any sense."

"Because of what I did?"

"Because of what you did. You keep saying these things that don't match up with what you did. So stop pretending that things ended any different way than they actually did."

Just then, the waiter comes with our menus.

"I think we're about ready to order," Landon tells the bald, big-nosed man.

"Oh?"

"She'd like the flank steak with roasted potatoes and green beans, and I'd like the same, please," he tells the waiter.

Um, what now?

He grins at me as the waiter leaves. "How'd I do?"

I almost want to call the waiter back and change my order just to wipe that self-satisfied smirk off his face, but I really do want the flank steak.

"Listen, I know I was a dick back in college," he says. "But I meant what I said before. I really am sorry."

"You weren't just a dick." I have to force myself not to raise my voice. I've been waiting over nine years for this long-overdue apology. Let's just say emotions are running high. "You broke up with me in the middle of a party, in front of everyone - Pamela, your brothers, all our friends, random people we hardly knew. Then, you just left. No explanation. Nothing. Just yelling 'I don't want to be with you anymore, get it!' and rushing out. Then you disappeared. No calls. No texts. Nothing. Three years down the drain."

Landon rakes his hand through his light brown hair. "It was a douchebag move."

"And you never told me why," I continue, getting angrier and angrier the more I speak. I know I should stop, that the time to stop was minutes ago, but I can't. Fuck Landon. And fuck me, for even agreeing to come here with this jerk, no matter what he said. "One day things seemed perfect, the next I was single with an ex who didn't even have the decency to tell me why."

Landon can't meet my eyes, is scowling. "I was just a stupid kid, and I..."

His jaw tightens. "Forget it."

"You're not going to tell me why," I say dully.

"It doesn't matter," he says. "OK? I... I don't want to talk about it. Point is that you didn't deserve that, at all. I'm sorry. I don't blame you for hating me."

"OK," is all I can say.

"Kyra - " he begins.

"Listen," I say. "You lost the right to be with me years ago. But if you stop being an ass, we can maybe be... not enemies. OK?"

He nods, exhales. "OK. I can live with that."

"Good. Because there are some things you don't get second chances for. Marrying your sister's ex-husband. War crimes. Breaking up with your girlfriend in front of all your friends without a damn reason why."

Landon chuckles. "That's on the same level as war crimes?"

I find myself chuckling too. "Well. You know what I mean."

"I do." He shrugs. "No argument here. I deserve it."

And, just like that, a tension that was hovering over the table lifts. Our conversation gets easy, simple, like with any old friend, but better. Our steak gets delivered, and our red wine too. We eat and drink and talk.

When I'm not thinking about what a dick Landon can be, he can actually be pretty fun. He's jokey, irreverent, and a great conversationalist. We talk about his travels to Prague and the rest of Europe, how he's still working away at reading the whole Robert B. Parker series, how weird it is for him to be President of Storm Media when he always thought that would be Greyson's job.

"It still feels like some weird nightmare-dream," he confesses. "I mean the office - it's Dad's old office - I try to stay away from it. It's... too much. Doesn't feel like mine. Every time I try to even slightly move or shift anything, it feels wrong. Nah, I spend most of my time in my old office, which has all my stuff in it. But God, Kyra, you should see the place - all of Storm Media's offices now. Dad did some renovations a few years back, and it's all windows and sleek modern furniture. He even added some foosball tables and a jungles' worth of tropical plants in the break room. Almost makes me feel like I'm working for Google."

"You're not giving any tours, are you?" I joke.

"Actually..." A dangerous smile comes over Landon's face as his blue eyes ensnare mine. "There's a tour going on tonight."

"Oh?"

"It's a very exclusive, very private tour."

"What about the tour guide?" I say, smirking as I play along.

"Just some guy. The important thing is: you're invited."

By now, we've finished our meal and dessert. We've been lingering at the table, just talking.

I feel light, up for anything.

"Now?" I ask.

"Now," he says.

Don't you dare - this is a bad, a very bad idea, I think.

"OK," I say.

His mouth parts in delighted surprise. "Yeah?"

"Yeah. But it better be free."

"Of course." He's already rising, looking around for our waiter. Then he winks at me. "Although we do accept tips."

Which is how, twenty minutes later, I come to be standing before the door of the offices of Storm Inc. I can't help but think how close I probably am to all the evidence I need to nail them on the plagiarism charges. Surely Colin Storm's journals are squirreled away here somewhere. But the next thing I know, Landon's whisking me inside, pointing out ten things at once. "And over there is our state-of-the-art coffee machine, which can make about five at once, and espresso, and some weird latte thing I think is crap, but Nolan loves. And over there is..."

I let his voice fade to the back of my consciousness as I take it all in. The renovations really were an improvement. The full-wall windows and sleek chrome furniture are gorgeous. It almost feels like a spread in an interior-decorating magazine, or even an Ikea set-up, rather than a real office that has people in it five or however-many days a week.

"And here we are," he says, coming to a stop.

Somehow, we've made it all the way to his office without me noticing.

It's smaller than the one he quickly showed me as his father's. Has a glass desk and a black leather chair that looks big enough for two.

The door is closed behind us.

Landon goes over to sit down, turns himself around a bit. When I finally let myself look at him, I find he's looking right at me.

Hello there, heat between my legs.

"So, this is where it all happens," I say in what I hope is a light voice.

I try to think of an excuse to leave, but my mind is blurry, blank.

His gaze says it already, but then he says it aloud in a hoarse voice: "Come here."

"Landon," I say, rooted to the spot.

I can't leave. I can't stay.

My fists are balled at my sides.

Idiot.

What else did I think would happen, coming here? Even if talking to him was as easy and fun as ever, at the end of the day, he's Landon Storm. He takes what he wants.

God, how could I have let myself forget that?

It seems an eternity, him rising, coming over to me, cupping my face with his hands. That gaze never so much as budging.

"Go away," I murmur.

"Alright," he says, and then he kisses me.

It's soft and giving and a question, one that my body answers instinctively. I pull away - and then, as if I'm a boomerang, give in.

Yes...

Our lips meet and remeet with a rightness that's old. Kissing him is in its own category. The way his tongue guides mine. How his hands wrap around me, hold me and stroke me so tightly that I find myself trembling.

Oh... fuck.

Pull away - I have to. The last of my self-control is ebbing away. But every new kiss, every stroke, every action of his produces an equal and opposite reaction in me - one that can't be avoided.

I've wanted this for so long. Missed this. Needed this.

He tips his forehead to mine and, eyes meeting mine, murmurs, "I've been wanting to do that for too damn long."

CHAPTER 7

Landon

Kyra's eyes narrow into a glare, although the corners of her mouth stay turned-up, teasing. "One week is too damn long?"

Shit. Why did I say that? Even if it was true, how could I be idiot enough to think that saying it would lead to anything good?

It's just that when I'm with Kyra, I forget myself. Forget everything else.

"Longer than that," I admit, ending it off with a kiss.

Fucking hell do her lips feel good against mine. Her tongue is the perfect partner, too, the yin to my yang. She gives and she takes. She follows and she leads.

Yes, this is the same Kyra who was my girl all those years ago - but she's different, too.

Our fingertips enmesh, lift over each other. I kiss her to the wall and pin her there.

Her eyes are half-lidded - with pleasure, with a bit of anger, who knows. All I know is where I want to be: inside her.

"Landon," she says suddenly, pushing me away.

I pause, even though I can feel, like a magnet, a force pulling me right back to her. I need to touch her, kiss her. Be with her.

"Just not enemies," she says, narrowed eyes scanning my face.

"Just not enemies," I repeat, ignoring the weird wrench in the pit of my gut.

"Good," she says.

And then she kisses me. This kiss is different from before - more uninhibited, holding nothing back. I find my hands going under her ass, picking her up. I walk her over to my chair, sit her down.

I spangle kisses along her neck, using a bit of teeth. She groans, her hands exploring the contours of my muscles.

I unzip her dress. She pauses. Our eyes lock.

Can she feel it - the urge practically ripping me apart - to take in every bare bit of her, commit it to memory, take it, enjoy it, claim it for myself?

All I know is that she's wearing way too many clothes. I strip her bare.

Dress, then bra, then panties. Then - I can't help it - I stand there and enjoy her.

"You finished yet?" she says with a smirk.

"Not nearly," I growl.

My lips refind hers, my hands her breasts. Wow. They're just as I remembered - only better. All of her is. Her curves, the light freckles on her shoulders, the devilish curl of her pouty-lipped smile.

How could I ever have been OK with not seeing this again, not having it to myself?

Of course, the plan was never to...

Stop. I can't let myself go there. She's here now, with me now. That's the important thing. The only thing.

She tastes like the chocolate cake we ate, and smells like some sort of berry I'd die happy eating.

My face nestles against her breasts, and I inhale her scent. Then, my mouth suctions onto a nipple.

"Landon," she groans.

Goddamn do I love the sound of my name in her mouth. I want more of it.

I pinch her other nipple and she groans again. I'm rock-hard and she hasn't so much as touched my cock.

Lips and tongue work together to suck her breast, my hand enjoying the round firmness of the other.

Then my hands wander down and we freeze. Fuck. This is it.

Our gazes meet.

Hers says: Dare you.

Oh, I dare.

"Landon," she groans again as my fingers skid across her opening.

"Fucking wet as fuck," I growl with approval.

The only question is... is her pussy...

My fingers go in and a pleased grunt rolls out of me. Yep, as responsive as ever. As I finger her, Kyra sinks back into the chair, head rolled back.

Hell yeah is that what I like to see. I finger her fast and hard and rough, as moan after moan falls out of her mouth. Her lips are slack, panting.

"Oh yeah?" I say, and when her whole body starts shaking, I can't take it anymore.

I rip off my pants, turn her around and shove myself inside her.

It's... oh. Fuck. Fuck. Fuck.

There are no... fuck... words.

Fucking perfect. Her clasping at me.

I can only fuck her slow it's so good. Too good. Any faster and I'd...

Landon. Concentrate.

But I fucking can't. She's too fucking hot. Too fucking good. Fuck. Fuck.

And the way she's groaning.

I pick her up, still inside her, and bend her over the desk.

"Still hate me?" I growl into the back of her neck.

As I pause, her pussy clasps at me franticly.

"I will if you stop," she hisses back.

That's all the go-ahead I need to start pounding her as hard and fast as I've got. In and fucking out. Just right. Just so good.

Her moans have become shrill whines, and now she's screaming. As she loses it on my dick and comes, I hold mine in. No fucking way am I letting myself come. Not yet.

I'm going to give her a night she won't soon forget. A night she'll ache to repeat.

I've been waiting to do this for too long.

I keep on pounding her, slower and deeper this time. Her whole body trembles with every insertion.

"Landon..." she groans. "Yes..."

"You sure?" I pause, enjoying how into this she is far too much. "Because if you really hate me..."

She twists around to glare at me, mouth parted with hunger. "I hate you. Now fuck me."

That's all the permission I need to fuck her senseless.

Although she's lying. Has to be. The way she's losing it with me, the places she's going with me as I fuck and fuck and fuck her - it's places reserved for something else.

When she screams out my name and comes for the third time, I let myself lose it too.

Fuck is she good. Fuck is this good.

And afterwards, on my cushy leather office couch, I hold her in my arms and nothing in the world feels better.

**

At some point in the morning, half-asleep, I notice she's still in my arms. Almost on autopilot, my mind starts running through the facts:

- Kyra's asleep in my arms.
- I actually like it.
- She's hot as hell.
- We passed out on the couch in my office.
- I have no idea how she's going to be when she wakes up.
- Does she still hate me?
- Breakfast?

I have the perfect one in mind: I'll make pancakes. That was always her favorite brunch food - and I even have frozen wild blueberries to top it off.

My stomach growls happily. Pancakes sound damn good right about now, but first I need... sleep. Yes.

Some nice... sleep...

**

I wake up cold. The Egyptian cotton sheets are around me and yet... My eyes snap open. My arms are empty.

She's gone. Left.

I check my phone, then the en suite bathroom, but there's nothing.

Fuck. She's gone without so much as a goodbye.

CHAPTER 8

Kyra

I'm making Madison some melted cheddar cheese on a cinnamon raisin bagel when his first call comes.

"Mommy, do you have a big case?" she asks, before I finally turn off my stupid phone.

"You bet," I say.

The two of us are at the park, me pushing her on the swings - "Wheee! Look at me, Mommy!" - when the second call comes.

By the time the third one comes, Madison is playing Beanie Baby war in her room, and I pick up.

"What?"

"Good afternoon to you too," Landon says.

"OK. I'm a bit busy right now."

"What about later tonight?"

"Yeah, I'll be free."

I can't let myself think - about last night, about him calling me up today. I just have to get off the phone. Get back to my daughter.

"Great - see you then," he says easily.

"Hold on, what?!?"

"I'll swing by," he says, as if my agreement is a given. "There's this thing I'm planning on booking for us..."

"Landon."

"What?"

"Last night was a mistake."

"That's one way of putting it."

Despite myself, I smile. God, the man can be a stubborn bull sometimes.

"Another way of putting it," he continues, just as confidently, "would be: awesome. Amazing."

"OK." I roll my eyes. "An awesome, amazing mistake."

He chuckles. "Can anything that's awesome and amazing really be a mistake, though?"

"Listen, Landon," I say. "I'm not going to sit here and argue semantics with you. You said that after the date you'd leave me alone - so are you going to keep your word or not?"

Madison lets out a laugh so delightedly loud that I can hear it through her closed door. I find myself smiling again. I've really never met a kid who enjoys playing alone as much as she does.

I drum my fingers on my wrist absently. Landon still hasn't answered.

The silence is unnerving. After waking up in his arms on his office couch, I hurriedly got dressed and rushed home, and I've been with Madison ever since. It's been good. Perfect. No time to think about it. What I've done. But now...

"So that's it," Landon finally growls.

"I've got a case against you," I say. "This complicates things."

"Then don't make it complicated."

"It's not that easy, and you know it."

"All I know is that I want to see you tonight."

"Well, you can't."

"When can I see you, then?"

"The next court date is Monday. I'd advise you to bring your A-game. We're finding more evidence every day."

That part is a bit of a stretch, but there's no harm in putting a bit of fear in him.

"When can I see you, outside of court?" he insists.

My finger twitches - I've been gripping my phone so hard that my fingertips are red. Shit, how can this be happening? How am I getting involved with Landon again, after all the promises I made to myself, after how he hurt me?

"Kyra," he says, "just come out with me again. See where it leads."

I sink to the floor, staring straight ahead of me. How am I supposed to say no? How can I, when every part of me is screaming yes?

"Kyra," he says, more softly. "Please. Just one more time."

Just one more time - famous last words. And yet ones I can't seem to disagree with.

I open my mouth to say no, and what comes out is: "Fine."

"Lunch?" he asks.

"Sure. We can see if we can do it like normal people."

"Challenge accepted," Landon says before hanging up.

I sit there for too long and feel sick and tired and excited and energetic all at once. I want to smack my head against the wall and skip down the hallway. I'm a grown woman, a mother - and I'm being an idiot.

But then Madison peers her head out, and I get up.

The rest of the day is more fun and activities with Madison. We make paper lanterns together, whip up some chocolate chip cookies together, go to the pet store and enjoy the funny-looking fish together. She really brings out the best in me.

She's got her father's eyes and my sass and... Stop it. I'm not going to go down that mental road.

At night, I'm relaxing in front of an episode of Planet Earth with some Orville Redenbacher's when the phone rings. It's Pamela.

"Something's up," she declares.

I groan. Sometimes I really do think she's psychic.

"You haven't returned my call," she continues, and I groan.

"Crap, Pompom, I'm so sorry. I've just been strapped with Madison and this big case, haven't been thinking straight."

"You're seeing him," she continues. "Aren't you?"

"Huh?"

"Don't 'huh' me. I knew you getting into this case against Landon was a recipe for disaster."

"It's not like that," I say, then sigh. Who am I kidding, anyway? I might as well tell her - she is my best friend. I'd just been hoping to keep it under wraps for a bit longer, figure out what I actually think about it.

"What is it like, then?" she asks in a terrible light voice.

"OK, so we slept together," I say, "But it's nothing serious. We're still just figuring things out."

God, I even sound like a delusional idiot to my own ears.

Worst of all, Pompom is dead silent.

"I know," I say with a sigh. "But after he helped me out with the ride the other day, then he insisted on this dinner at Balsac's, and we ended up touring his office and... That happened."

"Well, it could be worse," she says. "You could've ended up with Crazy Rory."

"Thanks," I say.

Crazy Rory is one of Pompom's date horror stories - he ended up locking them both in his bedroom and refusing to let her leave since 'they' were watching and 'they' would question her for everything she knew about him.

"Listen," I say, "I know it was a stupid move, a mistake, but it's too late now. It happened. And I have to deal with it."

"Are you seeing him again?" she asks.

That's Pamela for you - cutting right through the shit. Maybe she has a silly nickname from her love of wearing hats with pompoms, but she sees things how they are.

"Just tomorrow," I say.

"Why?"

"I don't know," I say, even though I do.

"You're giving him another chance?"

"I don't want to think about it right now!" I exclaim, surprised at the vehemence in my voice. "Listen, Pompom, I don't need you to tell me that this is a bad idea, or to remind me what a dick Landon was - but he apologized, and I tried to resist, but this all just happened. And if I sit around being miserable and beating myself up about it, then I'm not going to be able to concentrate on this case or being a good mom. OK?"

"Got it," Pompom says. "Lips are sealed. But you still have to give me details. How was the dinner?"

"Amazing," I admit, pausing.

Surely, there's a way to explain it to Pamela, make her understand: our high-up spot in the most beautiful building I'd ever been in, the delicious food, the whirlwind tour after, how all of that paled when compared to the happy slant of his smile.

"Down for a movie night?" Pompom asks, breaking me out of my thoughts.

"Of course." I chuckle. "Couldn't you have just asked that first and we could talk about all this in person?"

"Nah." I can hear the grin in her voice. "I wanted details first. I'll be there in 10."

"See you!"

**

Next morning, he calls me just as I'm about to get Madison up and going. "Thought I'd give you a heads-up - the hearing for today's been postponed. My lawyer has started digging out Dad's files and wants me to take a look to see if she's missed anything."

"Oh." Is the settling in my chest relief or disappointment? I do love my job. "OK. Thanks for the heads-up."

"We still on for tonight?"

"OK," I say. "Just..."

"What?"

"It's all happening so fast."

"OK."

"Well..."

"What do you want me to say?" he growls. "That I'm sorry for what happened? Because I'm not. I'm glad I kissed you. I'm glad I took you out. I'm glad we slept together. All of it was great, and I want to see you again. What's wrong with that?"

"Nothing," I say.

Except that I don't want to be hurt again.

"Listen," he continues, "how about this: we meet up at the park, no pressure, just have a nice time together as friends. That OK?"

"Yeah," I find myself saying, "that sounds perfect."

"Great," he says. "Seven PM at Central Park?"

"Mom?" Madison says, padding into the kitchen in her bare feet and nightgown.

"One sec," I mouth to her.

"I've got to go," I tell Landon, "but yeah, seven works."

"Angry mailman?" Landon jokes.

"Goodbye," I say, then hang up.

I draw Madison into a hug - though it's more for me than her.

Close one, is the thought that comes to mind.

Ugh - close one what? Close to revealing to Landon that I have a daughter, like I should've done days ago?

I take a breath. Whatever I should or shouldn't have done, I'm here now with my daughter. It's time to get ready for school. Time to put Landon and all that aside. It's time for me to be present here with my daughter - 100%.

An hour of Cheerios, tooth brushing - "That wasn't five minutes, Maddy!" - lunch packing ("Not carrots again, Mom!"), and we're ready to go. Maddy bounces out of the car as eagerly as usual, although this time, she pauses. "Mom?"

"Yes, honey?"

"Is being an adult as fun as being a kid?"

I pause, caught between a chuckle and a sigh. Sometimes Madison says such surprisingly insightful things, it just about bowls me over.

My first instinct is, "Of course, Maddy," but then I get to thinking. I made a promise to myself a long time ago that I would only lie to my daughter when absolutely necessary - Santa, the Easter Bunny, stuff like that. Right now, even if the truth isn't as happy as I'd like it to be, it still is the truth. Madison deserves the truth.

"It's different," I say. "Complicated."

Maddy nods. "So, it's not."

"I didn't say that."

"It's OK, Mom."

And with that, she leaves. I watch her skip off, waving to a friend.

And here we have Instance 57 of failed parenting...

But what should I have said? That it's fun in different ways, and even more fun sometimes, but it's more painful and scary too, because it's often the adult hurts that take the longest to heal. That we don't have to fear knee scrapes and monsters under the bed, but harm from much vaguer sources.

Someone behind me honks.

Right - my kid is long gone into the school. Time for me to go.

I head over to Starbucks. There, with my Grande Latte with extra cinnamon, I camp out in my usual corner booth with my laptop and do a bit more research for the case, call up a few colleagues. Normally, I'd let myself rest on all the evidence we have already, but this time I want to make sure that my time with Landon hasn't messed with my professional judgment. That I'm not banking on a slam dunk for a case that's still at the free throw line.

I keep my phone at the edge of the table, behind my laptop, out of sight. If only I could keep it out of mind.

Landon's already texted twice.

I haven't responded. I can't seem to send him the text calling off tonight.

I have literally no excuse - Madison already has a sleepover scheduled at her friend Annie's house, so all I have to do is drop her off and not worry for the rest of the night - other than the real one: I'm still not sure what we're doing is right.

And yet, time ticks along, and even though I haven't responded to his earlier three texts, when Landon texts me See you in 10?, I respond, See you in 20.

Next comes closing my laptop, throwing out my cup, going into the bathroom to change into something more date-y, and leaving Starbucks with more bounce in my step than I should.

Once I'm in my car pulling out onto the street, even catching a glimpse of a particularly poofy poodle prompts a smile.

If I didn't know better, I'd think I was starting to fall for him.

But I do know better. I know what Landon's capable of. I know how far this can go - and how far it can't.

I know how far this is from a good idea.

And still, I keep driving for it, this unavoidable conclusion.

After I've parked, I walk to where we arranged to meet: Trefoil Arch, Central Park.

Before he sees me, I take a few good moments to admire him. The nice light blue polo shirt he fills out to perfection. The tanned sculpt of his features.

Those dark eyebrows of his are lowered, the way they do when he's lost in thought.

When he glimpses me, his whole face transforms. Lifted eyebrows, wider smile, even his eyes change in a bunch of infinitesimal ways I couldn't pin down if I tried. You can't fake a smile like that.

"This old place," Landon says with a chuckle as I approach, although he only glances at the twist of tall grass and bulrushes before his gaze settles back on me. "Do you remember..."

"Of course."

"First kiss," he says. He steps towards me, gaze on his goal: my lips. "Why not..."

I put my hands against his chest. "Landon."

He stops, forehead crinkling in confusion.

Damn it, how is he still hot even when he's confused?

Looking away, I take a breath to regain control of myself.

I will not let him dictate how today goes. I will not.

"Weren't you the one who agreed to come here as friends?" I remind him in a voice that's way steadier than I'm feeling.

Chill, you're at a park. Yes, you slept together, but you can still be in control. Maybe.

"Hmm." He grunts. "Doesn't sound like me."

Under my glare, he starts to chuckle. "OK, OK. Just forgot."

"No problem," I say.

My gaze scans over his shoulder for another focus, anything other than the demand in those eyes.

"You look great, by the way," he says.

"I was working," I say, offhand, as if I hadn't changed into this yellow and black sundress in the cramped Starbucks bathroom before heading over here.

Ah, I know where I can go.

"Goodbye?" he asks as I start to head for it.

"Alice. Haven't seen that statue in centuries."

He follows along, frowning.

Maybe it was rude, me just walking off without so much as a 'come join', but him 'forgetting' about what we talked about wasn't exactly the epitome of politeness, either. Even if my heart is still offbeat from our almost-kiss.

"So," he says, as he walks alongside me. "How are things with you?"

"Things being my life or things being the case?" I ask lightly.

His scowl deepens. Goddamnit, the man is even hotter when he's pissed. Fuck me. "You."

"I'm fine. Just didn't sleep great last night."

"Yeah, me neither." He says it with a swinging gaze my way that indicates I'm to blame.

Another flicker of oppositions in me: arousal and annoyance. Arousal that I've gotten into his head enough to have him losing sleep over it. Annoyance that he actually expects me to feel bad over it. This whole thing has been his train - if he doesn't like where it's heading, then tough.

I give my head a little shake. Enough obsessing over the man.

I reorient my gaze to my surroundings, forcing myself to really take them in. The trees are in their full summery splendor. We're walking under a near-ceiling of rustling lime leaves that's chittering with life: fat grey squirrels, teeny chipmunks - there's even a blue jay eyeing us with a tilted head. Lilacs as tall as basketball nets waft their perfume all over us.

I inhale, can't quite stop an oncoming smile.

Ah yes, here we are.

The paths are as empty as I'd have liked them to be if we really were what we look like, the way my arm's hooked in Landon's (when did that even happen? Old habits...) - young, shy lovers off on a new adventure.

No, this rodeo is old, even if it doesn't feel like that - and I'd rather these romantic shady paths be crowded with people, rude, noisy, horrid people who would be a useful distraction, annoyance, anything.

"Ah, here we are," I say, letting go of his arm as we approach the bronze statue that's as high as a building.

It's bigger than I remembered, more detailed. You can see every hair in Alice's wispy eyebrows, every ripple on the bow the grotesque-looking Mad Hatter is wearing.

"You really read the book?" Landon says.

"You remembered?" I ask.

"Didn't you have this idea in college..." He's squinting, trying to remember, half-smiling with it. "An Alice in Wonderland themed club: loopy drinks and wacky music, toadstool tables and Alice herself presiding over the bar?"

"It was just a silly idea," I say quietly.

"I know, I know. Especially for a serious law student with her whole logical life ahead of her."

When I don't say anything, he continues, "I actually thought it was kind of cool."

"You laughed at me." I won't look at him - I won't. "And you are now too!"

"No, I'm not." His hand catches mine.

I pull away. "Well, you should. There's already a bunch of tea houses and bars themed like that already."

"So it wasn't such a bad idea then."

"Maybe not. But life happened."

"I know. You were a dedicated student. And it shows: you're killing us in there."

"I'd rather not talk about that."

He falls silent, which is good, although I wasn't really being honest.

While it feels wrong, us mentioning the case, what feels wronger is dancing around the truth, how I have from almost the start.

Madison. The real reason I never went ahead with the bar idea. The reason I almost didn't make it through law school, and wouldn't have without Mom's help.

The reason, right here, right now, I feel like doing nothing more than turning my back on this man and leaving without looking back.

You have a daughter, I remind myself. A goddamn beautiful, amazing daughter, who's the best thing you've ever created. Tell him. Tell him.

But telling would mean meeting, would mean... no, not yet. Not now. Probably not ever.

Which means this, me and Landon - this can never happen.

But for now, whatever this is, for now, maybe.

"Fancy a bit of boating?" Landon asks.

"I'll be doing the rowing," he adds a few seconds later, suddenly surly.

"You will?" I ask. "I haven't even agreed yet."

His scowl darkens. "There's your MO: arguing with everything I suggest."

"It's my job to argue," I point out.

"That makes it OK?"

"I didn't say that."

"Then what are you saying?"

At some point, we got close and all up in each other's faces, and I'm only now noticing. How his full lips are parted, ready for what I can't let happen. How his hazel eyes look greener when he's mad - or is it when he's aroused?

I take a step back, swallow. Chill, Kyra. "I'm saying that I wanted - want - to go slow - and you..." I trail off, sighing in exasperation at the look on his face. As convincingly innocent as it gets. Damn him. Now I remember why this all seems familiar. "You just suggested we do another date you always promised me we'd do when we were together."

Landon can't even fully scowl anymore. "Fair."

"Thanks."

He steps forward. "Is that a no?"

"No, it's a... let's see if any are available. Paddle boats are pretty popular with tourists."

"Who said it's a paddle boat?"

"Oh, I'm sorry, did you manage to squeeze a cruise ship in here?"

We chuckle at that. "No, no, you got me. We'll have to save cruising for later. I wish I could've gotten my sailboat here - but we can do that another time somewhere else."

We'll have to save cruising for later... Another time, somewhere else... My sailboat... why does he have to keep making plans and trying to impress me as if we have a future together? Or does he not realize what he's doing?

Why do I even care?

Talk about overthinking things.

The Loeb Boathouse terrace is striped tan and lined mahogany, but there's no one underneath it. No one but a tan, breezy man who tells us that of course we can have a boat.

So much for that last-ditch hope.

"That'll be $75," the man says.

I've almost gotten out my card when Landon hands his over to the man.

"Hey," I say.

"Hey," he says.

"I want to at least split," I say.

"Why? To underscore that this isn't a date?" He makes a face as he taps his card. "Fine, this isn't a date. Happy?"

"Not really, no," I say, although I put away my card.

By now, I know that there are some things you don't fight with Landon about.

He pats my shoulder. "Don't worry - a few minutes out on the lovely lake and you will be."

Turns out, it's not a few minutes - it's five - but yes, Landon was totally right.

Who couldn't be happy with the lake lapping its seaweed-scented breath against the sides of our boat, the rhythmic splash of Landon's paddling ("No," he said simply, with an irreverent smile, when I asked if I could help), the far-off cry of a seagull or two?

Who couldn't be happy with the passing Central Park views, all private and singular and communal all at once: the big-hatted Spanish woman with the fluffy white kitten in her arms, the two bathing-suit-clad blonde toddlers splashing each other in the pond. A family of ducks swimming past, heads at an erect, self-important angle.

Landon says nothing.

Who knows, maybe he gets it. That now is the kind of time, here is the kind of place that words only get bunched up around.

"There it is," Landon says softly after a few minutes, at my ear. "Caught ya, happy girl."

With the tips of his fingers, he traces the outlines of my lips. A shiver goes through me.

"What are you going to do about it?" I ask softly.

Hand under my chin, he turns my head to face his. "Take my payment."

A kiss follows next, is the only thing that could. His lips, my lips, our lips fuse into one. One outflowing. One perfection.

The water laps and a breeze sprays us with dandelion seeds.

Landon breaks away to sneeze, then laugh. Sneeze-laugh.

I laugh too. "Still allergic?"

He heaves a sigh. "Haven't got the dandelion vaccine yet."

And we laugh again, and, of course, it's so delightful - all of this - and him too - the man who made it all happen - it's so funny and wild and amazing, that we have to do the best expression of it, the celebration - our lips, his hands on my face, my hands against his chest.

Him, and him, and him.

Yes.

When he finally pulls away, there's something strained in the clench of his features. "My place?"

And just like that, the magic's lost.

"We've been here barely an hour," I say, trying to keep my voice steady. It's OK, not a big deal. "Unless you never intended to stay?"

"No." He swallows. "Just... got carried away. I was enjoying myself."

"I was too."

We eye each other like it was the other that betrayed us. Maybe I'm being oversensitive - probably. But everything was so perfect, and then he had to...

What? Want to spend more time with me?

No. Get to what I fear this was all about. Him and me, in bed. Even if we didn't work on paper, in real life, in bed, our bodies together, everything got sorted out. Easy. Wrong was made right.

What if all this was just a means to an end, a path to the only destination he cared about?

"Kyra," he's saying now.

"Yeah?"

"I'm sorry. I didn't mean... Just, you know, I can't exactly tear off your clothes right here."

"I get it," I say.

"Do you? That when I'm with you I lose control?"

Something I could've said.

"What about this," he says. "I paddle you around some more - there's a cove I've heard good things about. Then, if you feel up to it, we can go for ice cream. Today can end there - if you want it to."

I can't help but smile. "You're really bringing your A game today."

"I don't have a B game."

I lean in to give him the lightest of kisses. "No. You don't."

When I pull away, there's an odd look on his face. "Although there is something I want to tell you."

My heart drops.

CHAPTER 9

Landon

"You're beautiful," I say, and lean in to kiss her.

Laughing, she gives me a playful smack. "You're the worst."

I give a half-shrug, smirking.

Then I keep on paddling. It helps keep my mind clear. Or clearer, anyway.

Goddamn is she beautiful.

I keep fucking putting my foot in my mouth. Or maybe she's just jumpy. She has a right to be.

All I know is that I'm kicking myself for saying I'll paddle her around some more, when all I really want to do is kiss her. And kiss her. And take her.

How am I supposed to keep my mind on our surroundings when she's dressed in that sundress - the tight in and out of her waist, the flaring around her generous hips. Were her breasts always so perfectly sized? I itch to touch her. Stroke her. Kiss every part of her.

But that will have to wait.

"You like it?" I ask, as I paddle us into the cove.

There's a gazebo on shore, and some flowers, and no one but us.

"I'm pretty sure about three different friends have done their wedding photos here," she comments with a chuckle.

"Looks the part," is all I can think to say.

I used to figure you were the girl I was going to marry, is all I can think.

Whoa. Where did that come from?

Maybe Kyra and I were great in bed - OK, definitely. Still.

Times have changed. I messed things up all those years ago. I'm lucky she's going along with even this.

Clearly, my head's getting screwed up from how fast things are progressing. Maybe Kyra wasn't far off with wanting to take it slow.

Too bad my foot's jammed on the gas.

"There's the ice cream," I say, pointing at a little stall truck in the park.

It's a bit earlier than I expected, but if I'm thinking crazy marriage thoughts, then I clearly need to get the hell out of this boat. And some food in my belly.

We dock on the shore, and I help her out, having to pry my gaze off her ass.

You'll get that later - if you're lucky.

Damn lucky, by the looks of it. As we head for the food truck, Kyra's quiet - usually a bad sign.

"You OK?" I ask her, hand automatically going to the small of her back.

"Yeah, I..." She trails off, nodding.

"Yeah?"

"Just, thanks." God is she pretty when she smiles. Pretty enough to kiss. "For all this, I mean. It's way better than I expected."

"What did you expect?"

She shrugs, laughs. "I don't know, a walk? Feeding the pigeons?"

"OK, that was one time, and that was with my grandfather, OK?"

"OK, OK." She's chuckling now, and I am too. Even as it dies down, I can't seem to stop smiling. "So."

At the ice cream truck now, I pause. "So. Mint chocolate?"

"Not anymore."

"Oh, so you have changed."

"You have no idea."

There's something sad in the way she says it. Why do I keep feeling like she's hiding something from me, something big?

Goddamn am I hungry.

"OK... double chocolate?" That was her second favorite, I'm pretty sure.

"Nope." A smirk. She's enjoying this, the little minx. "Guess again."

I groan. "Chocolate caramel? C'mon, I have to be close."

"Cherry," she says, half to me, half to the bored tween with earbuds in her ears manning the ice cream truck. Clearly someone's kid who got roped into doing this.

"Damn it," I say, "Who are you, even?"

A vicious grin that stirs my cock. "The lawyer who's gonna kick your ass in court."

Fuck yeah, if I could just get her over to the shady part of the park, the part that's thick with trees and brush where no one goes, just me and her, then kiss her again, kiss her hard and stroke off that hot little sundress...

"Hello?" Kyra waves a hand in front of my face. "Earth to Landon - you getting anything? Because all you're getting of mine is a bite."

Oh, I'll be getting much more of you - and you'll enjoy it.

"Mint chocolate," I tell the even more unimpressed tween, who's looking to the heavens, clearly thinking, 'This is my life and it's ending one minute at a time'.

Once I've paid - a quick, cute struggle for the machine has me grab Kyra by the waist and tap the card reader as she thrashes in my arms - Kyra shoots me a death look.

"If you can't in good conscience eat your ice cream, I understand," I say in a faux-grave tone. "And will take it off your hands."

Gaze on me, she takes a big, long lick of it that hardens my cock even more. "Not a chance."

She's enjoying this torture.

Linking my arm through hers, I get us walking. That should take my mind off things. A bit.

I lift my cone to toast hers. "To ice cream."

"To ice cream."

"I can't believe you don't like this anymore," I say as I devour mine. "Mint chocolate is the bomb."

"Correction," she says, lifting her cone to my lips, "cherry is the bomb."

I take a lick, then consider. "It is the semi-bomb." I lean in as she moves it away. "May need a few more licks to decide for sure."

She just laughs, pushing me away. "You've got your own."

I extend my cone out to her. "Which I'm happy to share with you."

She just shakes her head. "Some things don't come back."

"But some do," I say.

It's only when her gaze flickers my way that I realize we weren't talking about the ice cream.

I clear my throat. "So, about tonight."

"Not sure I can," she says.

"Oh?"

"I've got this thing."

"This thing."

It's there again, crackling in the air. This unsaid something.

I've never been a paranoid guy. Or even a particularly observant one. But I know this: there's something she's not telling me.

"I had a great time, though," she says quietly, finishing her ice cream.

How she ate it so damn fast is beyond me. Unless she planned her early exit all along.

"That your way of saying you want to go?" I say.

"You OK with that?" Her eyes are part challenge, part sad.

"Does it matter if I am?"

"No." She tosses the napkin and the end of her cone - ha, some things haven't changed - into the garbage.

"Alright. I'll walk you to your car."

"You don't have to."

"I'm not walking you to your car because I have to."

When I hold out my arm, she takes it. We walk in silence.

It's getting dark, almost night. The time of hot dates and wild nights out. Wonder which she's doing.

Or maybe it's back to the grind - how she used to back in the day, late nights in the library, studying.

When we get to her car, she looks so nervous and sad and yet kissable, those pouty lips, with the bottom one way fuller than the top, like they were crafted to kiss, that I can't help it. I kiss her.

She pulls away, trying not to look happier. But she is. I know I am.

"When you said we'd come here as friends... did you mean it?"

Her gaze is searching, and finds its answer long before I ask, "Is it so wrong to want to be with you?"

Her chuckle makes her whole face go sad again. Why is it that when I'm around her, half the time I can't land on the right thing to say? It's usually so easy for me.

"I don't know," she says. "It doesn't feel like it, but... I don't know."

She gets in her car, and, through the window pane, I can see her say, "Goodbye, Landon."

I watch her pull into traffic and drive away.

**

On my way back to my car, I check my phone. Nothing from her, but a few missed calls from Nolan, and a pissy text: You dead or what?

I call him up. "Not dead, sorry."

He sighs. "I was so enjoying the thought of inheriting Dad's green leather couch."

"Why?" I say. "You pass out on it often enough anyway."

He chuckles. "True. Speaking of - you down for Storm-ing the club at LAVO?"

"Greyson is too?" I ask, surprised.

Ever since he got married to Harley, he barely goes out. Other than that brotherly intervention the other day. Not that I blame him. He has a wife he loves, and a kid to look after. Clubbing doesn't exactly rank up there with those.

Not that it's a sacrifice I'd happily make. Kids are great and all, but I've seen too many friends devoured by the whole 'perfect parent' identity. Before you know it, they haven't had sex with their wife in months, are gabbing about how 'Anthony's just great with these Baby Einstein videos, he even learned to walk two weeks earlier than normal', and are genuinely oblivious to how little the rest of the world cares. Or maybe I'm just an emotionless monster.

"Hello? Landino?" Nolan says.

Huh. I've been zoning out a bunch today.

"Yeah?"

"I said no, but who needs him anyway? He's always scaring the hot ones off."

"By asking them what their intentions are?" I chuckle. "He's just making sure our baby brother Emerson doesn't get roped in again."

"That was his own damn fault," Nolan declares, chuckling himself. "Although Jesus, Cynthia was worth every penny."

"Say that to Emerson's savings." I shake my head. "How much did he lose on her?"

"Don't want to know," Nolan says. "I feel kind of extra-bad about it too, since I banged her after they broke up."

"Nolan."

"I know, I know. But I got back some of the cash she stole from Emerson, so it wasn't all bad."

"You martyr, you."

"OK, enough about me, though. How's the case going?"

"Shitty."

"And Kyra? You land that one in the bag yet?"

I'd almost forgotten. How this all started. Me bragging and being a tool with my brother. Now's my chance, though, because I have pulled it off.

"Nah," I say, to my surprise.

Why not tell him?

"Not surprised," Nolan says smugly. "Never seen a girl hate you as much as her. Although I don't think you were ever a bigger dick to anyone else. You're not the Lothario you think you are."

"Oh yeah?"

"Yeah - but maybe tonight you can prove me wrong?"

"Nah, you're right," I say. "Maybe I'm losing it."

Why not tell him?

"OK, cut the shit," Nolan says. "Seriously, man, I miss you. Let's go out tonight."

"I don't know. Not feeling it."

"Yeah, losing doesn't make me feel like the big man on campus either. Which is why we need to go out, get laid, and win. Like the good old days."

It does have its allure. Even only a few weeks ago, everything was so simple. I worked hard, played hard. Met hot girls, enjoyed them until I stopped.

And then came Kyra. Messing with my head.

"That a yes?" Nolan presses.

"That's a no," I say. "Let's do lunch tomorrow. Tonight, this loser needs sleep."

"Loser," Nolan whines.

"Loser," I shoot back.

"Congratulations, you're twelve."

"Congratulations, you, as my twin, are also twelve."

"I'm revoking our twinhood."

"What - really?"

Nolan sighs. "No. But I really wish you were coming tonight. Emerson is practicing this new Liszt piano piece, La Campa-something, and he won't shut up about it."

"Get him blackout drunk?"

"Obviously, but that'll take at least 30 minutes and a hundred dollars."

"Enjoy."

"Enjoy your piercing regret."

"Goodbye, Nolan."

"Night night, brother."

I hang up, frowning at the phone. Now that I think about it, tonight alone at home isn't exactly appealing. I can't remember the last time I've done it.

There's always been work to do, girls to see. Or just going out.

But tonight, there's nothing. Kyra was my plans.

Why did I say no? Why didn't I tell Nolan about Kyra and me?

Fuck it.

No good will come of thinking about it.

CHAPTER 10

Kyra

So that... just happened. My head is still spinning. It still feels like he's right beside me, scrambling my thoughts.

What I wouldn't give for one last kiss...

"That good, huh?" Pamela says knowingly, opening the front door of my place.

"Uh..."

She pulls me inside. "It's fine. I just called you to ask if you were OK with me reorganizing your shoe closet in the front - it's a horror, I found a stiletto inside your winter boot! - but then I heard your phone ring right outside and I realized you were standing right at the front door."

"Oh." I laugh. "Like a weirdo."

"Like a weirdo," she agrees, then, ruffling her lashes ludicrously, adds, "in looooove."

"Stop, please." I suddenly feel very, very tired. As if I was the one doing all the rowing today.

"I'm sorry. Maybe I shouldn't have let myself in, but you said you'd be home in 10, and it has been 20, so..." She gives me a side squeeze. "Anyway. Yeah. I know how intense this must be for you."

"And I know how much of an idiot you must think I am," I say, staring at my doormat that Mom knitted. Was that run in the purple stripe always there? "I know I do."

"Not an idiot, no," she says quietly.

"Then what?"

She shrugs. "You were each other's end game. I saw it then. I get it. Hard to let go of something like that. Especially when it comes back new and supposedly improved."

Key word supposedly.

"But if we were each other's end game, then what happened?" I ask her, though the question isn't just for her. It's for me, Landon, the Universe. "Why did he just dump me like that?"

"I don't know." Another shrug, although this one looks as sad as I feel.

She doesn't deserve to have this heaped on her, though, to have her whole night shadowed under the burden of what I'm putting myself through.

"Ice cream?" I ask her, already heading for the kitchen.

"You mind-reader," she says, grinning.

After all, you can never have too much ice cream.

**

The next day is some much-needed mother-daughter bonding time. After our favorite lunch - melted cheese on a bagel - Madison and I cover our hands in every color of paint from the 12-in-1 pack I got from Michaels - all the colors of the rainbow, and then some. We press and smear and goob different sheets of printer paper with swirls, hearts, happy faces, laughably misshapen cats and other animals.

As we're cracking up about our latest creation, a three-headed violet and lime turkey, it hits me: when she laughs, her hazel eyes crinkle just like his.

"Mommy?" Madison says, as I race for the bathroom.

"Be right back," I croak.

Inside, I brace myself against the sink, glare at my reflection.

You idiot. You stupid, stupid idiot. How could you have let this happen?

She doesn't have any answers, and neither do I.

All I know is that he's encroaching into my time with my daughter now, and it needs to stop. Maybe I shouldn't have left his texts this morning unread?

I stay there for another few minutes, until I've got my cool back.

A few stray thoughts about Landon aren't the end of the world. Even if I'd really, really rather they weren't there.

All that matters now is that Madison has a good rest of the afternoon with her mom, until it's time for a sleepover at Grandma's. Part of me almost wants to cancel, to have Madison to myself, but I know my mom looks forward to these weekly sleepovers basically as soon as Madison leaves her house the week before. She even plans out activities and what book she'll read Madison days in advance. I think she misses being a mom.

After me, her and Dad tried having more kids, but it was no dice.

At Mom's, Madison races into her cookie-smelling house, hollering, "GRRRAAAAANDMAAAAS!". After a big bear hug, Mom sends her into the kitchen for cookies, then gives me a careful, annoyingly knowing look. "You're still seeing that man."

"Mom."

She knows I don't want to go there with her. At all.

Last time I listened to her love advice, I got my heart broken. Maybe it wasn't her fault, but at any rate, I'm under enough stress right now without having her thinking I've lost it for dating Landon again. Or going on dates with him again. Whatever you'd call this.

"Well, you just have fun, dear."

"Mom." I give her another glare. "Tonight, it's going to be me and Pirate Johnny Depp."

"Oh." I can't tell whether she looks disappointed or pleased. Mom's had a tough time trusting men since Dad. "Well, you do know he's single now." A wink.

I roll my eyes, smiling. "Yeah, I'll get right on that, Mom."

As I walk away to my car, though, Johnny Depp is the last thing on my mind. The first is Landon.

Since I ignored his last two texts, he's sent a few more, plus called. Damn it, he's really not going to let this drop, is he?

Do you really want him to? an obnoxious voice in my head asks.

I drive home, hitting every red light, annoyingly. They sure do love me.

Pamela, I already know, is out on a hot date. 'How you should be too', she told me the other night. And she was right, and I even knew just the guy - Harvey, the high-level banker I met at a friend's wedding who is handsome, successful, kind, and who has already asked me out half a dozen or so times.

But I haven't wanted to get back into any serious dating these past few months with this big case, and I definitely don't now. Who am I kidding? As long as I keep seeing Landon, it would be unfair for me to see anyone else anyway.

At home, I clean up Madison's and my art mess. I do some laundry. I cook enough spaghetti Bolognese for the next four days. I even color-sort Madison's freaking closet and send Pamela a picture.

Then, I cave. I call him up. "Hey."

"Hey, busy girl."

"What's up?"

"Us, hopefully. If you're free?"

"I..." Think brain, think. There must be one thing more to do... anything. "...have to go grocery shopping."

"What a coincidence."

"Oh?"

"I love grocery shopping."

I can't help it: I laugh. "Landon."

"It's true. The free cookies, the new flavors of gelato they have every time I go, the bulk samples."

"I'm pretty sure the free cookies are for children."

"Don't worry - I'll get one for you too."

"Did I invite you along?"

Silence.

Shit. Why do I have to be so mean?

"I guess you could come," I say.

"I don't have to." A lot less enthusiasm in his voice now. "Don't want to pressure you into anything."

"You're not," I say. "Grocery shopping is fine. Myers, OK?"

"The one on Hudson? Sure. See you there in 20?"

"30," I say. "See you." I hang up.

After all, it's just grocery shopping. How hard can it be to keep my cool there?

I put on my coat before my mind can answer that question.

**

Landon's waiting for me inside the door of Myers, with an apologetic expression and two macadamia nut cookies. "Got here early. But figured I'd wait to enjoy mine until you got here."

I laugh, bite into it. It's damn good. "Thanks."

"I told them it was for my kid sister," he says.

"You are shameless."

Shrug. "It's for a good cause." A look swings my way. "You."

Two minutes in and I'm already thinking this is a poor, very poor, idea.

I give myself a little shake.

Cool it - just get the cart, look at your list, get the bread-veggies-meat-fruit-cookies-whatever. This is very, very doable.

How can his admiring gaze give me goose bumps in the middle of a freaking grocery store?

I get the cart and get shopping. Landon checks my list and comes back with almost half the items before I can even roll over to one.

"You know this place?" I ask.

"It's the one I go to," he says. "Decent prices, but still not too far."

"Well, thanks for your help," I say.

By the looks of it, we're nearly through the list. Which means I better have another excuse ready right about... now.

We make it through the checkout line with just some easy chitchat, though. Maybe this is enough for Landon. Maybe after this we'll go our separate ways and... I don't know. I'll have a nice night with Johnny.

That's not what you want, a nagging voice in my head butts in.

Shut up, I tell it.

As I go to pay, I joke to Landon, "No card war this time?"

He gets out his wallet. "Shit - if you want me to - "

"Stop." I tap my card. "I'm a big girl. I can buy my own groceries."

"Of course," he says.

Cute, how he actually looks sad he couldn't buy my groceries for me.

Once we're outside and I have my grocery bags on my arms, I smile at Landon. "Well, thanks."

There's a look in his eyes, one that I know from experience is dangerous. "Here's an idea," he says.

"I don't know," I say.

A frown. "I haven't said anything."

"Sorry."

He gestures to the store next door, Victoria's Secret. "It's Harley's - Greyson's wife's - birthday this weekend. Weird, but apparently, all she wants are PJs, so if you could help..."

"And you want my help because?"

"You're female."

We crack up. I roll my eyes. "Fine. But let me put this in my car first."

Inside the store, it's actually fun, going through the PJ sets: the ugly plaid ones and the cute plaid ones, the silly animal ones, the holy-hell sexy ones, until we come to ones that are way cute - pink penguins - without being wildly inappropriate - no lacey thong included.

"What is it?" Landon asks as we walk out of there.

I touch my face gingerly, realizing I've been grinning like mad.

"Nothing," I say.

"Right."

Although I'm full of shit and we both know it. I just don't want to say it, tell the truth:

That it felt like the good old days, when things between Landon and I were easy and uncomplicated and fun. When even standing in insanely long lines in the pouring rain was enjoyable - because he was there.

"That was fun," I admit, as he drops the stuff off in his car.

"Let me make it up to you," he says.

"You already did. Fair is fair. You went grocery shopping with me. I went girl PJ shopping with you."

"Kyra," he says softly.

"Can't we just leave it like this?" I ask, knowing that that's the last thing I want. That, even in a plain white tee and blue jeans, Landon looks fucking gorgeous. That all he has to do is ask me one more time and I'll cave. "A nice evening together?"

"I know a place," Landon says. "Let me take you there?"

A bit more of my self-control falls away with the look in his eyes. "Where?"

"The Baccarat Hotel."

"No."

"Restaurant first - see if we enjoy ourselves. Then, if we do, go from there."

Go from there... to the bedroom, the bed, the whole night... no.

I have to say it. I have to tell those hopeful eyes 'no', the lips already pouted for a kiss. I have to say it. Mean it.

"Landon," I say.

"Kyra," he says.

When I open my mouth, it's anyone's guess what's going to come out.

CHAPTER 11

Landon

"Fine," she says. "Just the restaurant, though."

I could kiss her now. But I know if I did I wouldn't be able to stop.

I've heard all I need to get driving anyway.

As I cruise down the road, I'm probably smiling like an idiot.

I, Landon Storm, am the luckiest fucking man in the world.

Beside me in the car, dressed in a slightly tight black button-up crop t-shirt and blue jeans, as hot as any supermodel in a designer dress that I've ever taken out - hotter even - is Kyra.

Her dark hair is pulled back in a messy ponytail, although she missed a strand. I want to tuck it in. I want to pepper the stripe of skin on her abdomen bared by her shirt with kisses.

Kyra, Kyra, Kyra.

I want to take her, right here, right now.

But first, dinner.

"I don't have anything to wear," Kyra blurts out as the skyscraper looms into view.

"Got you a little something," I say casually.

"Seriously, Landon?"

"Just stumbled on it the other day... Looked like your size."

Fuck. Why is it that those brown eyes are able to see right through me?

"What about you?" she asks.

"We can both change in the bathroom."

"I thought this was spontaneous, but... you planned this."

"It was just an idea. If the grocery shopping went well."

She holds my gaze, finally sighs. "Alright. But if it doesn't fit, I'm not wearing it."

"It'll fit, alright."

"Oh really? You're so sure, are you?"

I shrug. I'm not about to admit that I've just about memorized the shape of her.

When we hand over the car to the valet, I get out the bags of clothes, then we head into the bathrooms to change. I'm out of my old clothes and into my suit quickly enough, although I don't hurry out.

I want to see her and I don't. Every time I see her something happens to my brain. I get... 'stupid' isn't the word. But it isn't far off. Kyra always is one step ahead.

All I want to do is make her smile.

Fuck, I'm starting to sound like a fucking Hallmark card. Fuck that.

Outside, she's the first thing my eyes go to. Fucking hell.

What have I done?

"Hey," she says.

"So, it fit," I say, trying and failing not to let my eyes run all over her.

Wow. Fucking yeah.

The dress looked OK on the mannequin, but its bright red bands of material make her look like walking sex. Classy walking sex, but still.

A man with a stunner on his arm walks past, staring at Kyra. I glare at him.

That's my girl you're looking at, buddy.

"You look good," she says.

I take a breath. "Yeah, sorry. You too. Want to go in?"

She smiles, and then I have her hand in mine, and I can't tell if my pulse is racing because it's happening, we're going, or because she looks so damn happy.

That's my girl.

Inside is all red curved-ceiling, Art Deco, chandelier-filled splendor. Normally, I'd be admiring the decor, the Parisian style navy armchairs and hexagonal light wooden tables, but right now all I can admire is her.

I am a fucking idiot. I should've saved this dress for the bedroom.

I have a fucking boner and we haven't even kissed.

Right after we're seated, I order us some drinks.

"How do you know this place?" she asks.

"Dad used to have his Christmas parties here," I explain. "He'd spend as much as he could at the end of the year so he could write it off on his taxes."

"Sounds like your dad."

"Yeah," I say, eyeing her. "He always thought the world of you, though. Told me I was a damn fool when we broke up."

"Oh." She smiles a bit brokenly.

"Shouldn't have brought that up," I growl.

"No," she says.

"What about you, though?" I say.

"What about me?"

"I..." It's hard putting it into words. Especially with her looking so goddamn good across the table. "You've just changed so much. Feels like there must be a reason. A big one."

She sips her water, clearly even more uncomfortable. Looks like I'm on a fucking roll tonight. "Changed how?"

A shrug. "Sassier. Bolder."

She puts her cup down, eyeing me. "You know, I did a lot of growing up after you left me, Landon. There's... some things I should tell you."

"I know, and I was an idiot, a complete idiot." Am one now, seeing as I still can't bring my idiot ass to tell her the real reason, even as I'm seizing both her hands. "Really."

Her gaze drops to our clasped hands, just as the waitress putters up, at the worst time. "Here are your drinks."

"We're ready to order," Kyra blurts out, grabbing the menu, even though she didn't so much as glance at it earlier. "I'll have... steak."

"I'll have the steak too," I say.

Kyra takes a deep swig of her Sex on the Beach, and I drink my whisky on the rocks deeply too. I'm going to need it.

"So," I say.

"Sorry." Kyra forces a smile. "I'm hungry."

"Of course."

It takes me a good minute to figure it out: she's not going to tell me. It, or the 'things', whatever they are.

Although I have other things on my mind, too. "Tell me. What does a guy have to do to get you to stay the night?"

She leans in, the beginnings of a smile on her red lips. Were they always that red and juicy, or did she touch them up in the bathroom when she changed?

"We'll see," is all she says.

Overhead, there's a big band playing and, for the first time, over her shoulder, I notice a small crowd dancing.

"Look," I say.

She looks over her shoulder and laughs. "Wow. How did we miss that coming in? Looks like they're having fun."

"Want to join?"

"I don't know."

I rise. "I do. May I have this dance?"

The corners of her lips quirk up. Damn, do I want to kiss her. But this is second best. "Alright."

That 'alright' gets her off her seat, glides her onto the floor with me - it wraps our arms around each other's shoulders. Grooves our hips.

"Fuck," I mutter, suddenly remembering.

"What?" she asks.

"I hate dancing."

She just laughs. "This was your idea."

And yet, there's something about her hips moving with mine. Even as I step on everyone's feet. It makes it OK, fun even.

One song, then another. I can't seem to leave. I'm still a shitty dancer - all the moves, even as Kyra, laughing her head off, tries to show me, are as mysterious as if we're on an alien planet. But her grin just widens and widens, takes over her face. Takes me in, too. As long as she's smiling, I am.

Who knows how long has passed when our waitress taps me on the shoulder and gestures to our meals on the table.

Back at the table, eating, I say, "Phew."

"You were having fun, admit it," Kyra declares.

"I'll admit it. Though I didn't get any better. Admit that."

"I'll admit that," Kyra says.

We laugh.

Another drink, some chocolate pudding cake for dessert. Then, all at once, we're at the door, and I haven't asked the most important question of all. The only one that matters, really.

"Tonight?" I ask.

"Tonight," she answers.

And when we kiss, I finally figure out the meaning to what I'd always thought was a stupid phrase: takes your breath away.

**

"No," Kyra says, stopping in the doorway of the penthouse, her hand in mine. "No way."

I saunter in. Grin at our luxe surroundings: all white tones with a 360-degree view of the skyscraper-laden deep blue sky.

It's almost good enough for her. Almost.

"Yes way."

"I..." She looks at me carefully, a guarded look on her face that I hate. That I put there. "I can't accept this."

I shrug as I go to the couch to sit down. "I can't get a refund."

She goes to sit beside me, leans her head on my shoulder. "Thank you. For the dress, dinner, everything."

Her lips nuzzle mine. It's now. This is the moment.

I can finally give into the hunger ripping through me.

She tastes so good - like chocolate. Smells like vanilla. I can't stop looking at her, how beautiful she is, even when we kiss.

Opening her eyes slightly, she giggles. "Are you kissing me with your eyes open?"

"No," I bluster. "That would be weird."

She kisses me with a giggle. "Weirdo."

I chuckle, my hands going to the straps of her dress. "Not my fault with you wearing that dress - can't stand it on you a second longer."

Her mouth parts. "Oh?"

"Fuck yeah."

I pull it off her, toss it to the side. Then I rise.

"What are you doing?" she says, squirming.

I hold her in place, feast my eyes on her. "Let me look at you."

Hot as fuck. Those pale, milky-white curves. Those upturned tits with just the right amount of hang. I could eye-fuck her for hours.

Except she's here right in front of me and I'm hard as hell.

I sink to my knees, my lips going to one breast, then the other, then both. I press my face in between her full breasts and breathe in her scent.

Then, I kiss my way down as her groans grow louder.

"Been wanting to do this all night," I say between kisses. I lap and kiss and nibble at her upper thighs as her torso twists back and forth with pleasure.

And then my kisses and laps move to her opening, around it. My finger joins in, stroking and easing in. Her back arches.

"That's it." I dip my finger inside her. She's wet as fuck. "My Kyra."

Her eyes snap open. I have no right to call her that, but right now, there's nothing more that I want than to undo the past, make her mine for good.

The next best thing is now. My lips on her clit. My fingers inside her. I pulse and lap at her as her moans became one unending shrill.

Fucking right. I'm gonna pleasure her until she screams.

I pound her pussy hard as I swirl my tongue and lips around her clit. Her whole body's shaking.

"Jesus, Landon," she groans. "I'm... I'm..."

Seconds later, she's wailing and I know the answer already: she's coming. And it's fucking beautiful.

I keep on fingering and lapping at her, moving her from one orgasm to the next until she falls back, spent.

Afterwards, I lift her in my arms and carry her to the bed. Half-passed out, mouth still parted, she's gorgeous. She feels so good in my arms.

CHAPTER 12

Kyra

I come to in his arms. It feels so warm, so good, I almost don't want to stir. Or think.

That orgasm was so damn good. Everything with Landon was - is.

Jesus.

And his scent, musky and spicy, is making me want to curl up and never get up again.

What this man does to me...

But then my phone buzzes, and I remember.

Real life. Who I am. Who I'm responsible for.

It's just a spam email, some sexy Slovakian woman named Nina who apparently wants to be my wife, but I'm up now, getting more conscious by the second. Is it time to leave?

I don't want to, but... I'm not sure staying the night is the right choice either.

"You good?" Landon asks, a crease appearing between his eyebrows.

God, where to begin...

The concern in his eyes now.

How he pleased me just now...

He was always good in bed, before, but did he ever go down on me that damn good? Not just 'good', even. There's 'good' - and then there's the kind of good that lifts you into the stratosphere, outside of normal human experience. Him eating me out just now was that.

"You want to go," he growls, turning away.

"Landon."

"Say it, then." He rises, hands fisted at his sides. "Damn it, Kyra. I don't know how to win with you."

I'm being a bitch. A moody, indecisive bitch. Tonight, Landon couldn't have been any better. He bought me a gorgeous, expensive dress, dinner and booked us a hotel. What more do I want?

To erase the past, of course. Only it's impossible.

Anyway, I'm not being fair to him. Either I'm in this, or not. I can't just date him and then hold this massive grudge against him.

But how am I supposed to trust him again, when he betrayed my trust so completely before?

"I'm sorry," I say, my head on his back. "I want to stay. I'm just freaking out a little. And honestly, I can't promise that this - us - isn't going to freak me out. But I'm going to try my best not to let it ruin things. Is that enough for you?"

He turns to me. His face softens as he gives me a kiss on the forehead. "That's more than enough. I'm not going to disappoint you again. That's a promise."

Damn it. Aaaand I actually believe the man.

"Oh, I didn't show you the coolest part." Landon holds out his hand. There's an almost boyish excitement to his smile. "If you're game."

I grin. A smile like that is contagious. "First, I should probably get on some clothes."

"Hmm." Landon can't seem to pry his gaze off my naked body. "Seems a shame."

I giggle, reaching for my dress.

"Fine, fine," he says with a disappointed sigh.

He goes to the bathroom and comes back with a robe. "Though you won't be needing it for long... you'll see."

A minute or so later, after he's led me by the hand, I do.

"No way," I say, then laugh at myself. "Guess that's my go-to shocked phrase."

Landon kisses the corners of my smile. "As long as you like it."

I gesture at the dazzling set-up in front of us. "How could I not? Is there anyone on the planet who wouldn't like a private Jacuzzi with three walls and a floor of city views, along with a bottle of wine and bubble bath?"

"Someone who doesn't drink and is afraid of water?" Landon suggests.

We just chuckle and start the bath.

I step a bit away to gaze out the window, and hopefully hide my overawed face.

How is this my life, and how is it so awesome? The dress, the dinner, Landon, all these fun dates - the funnest I've ever had. Landon.

We just... work together. In a way that defies explanation.

"Tub's ready," Landon says, starting to shed his clothes, "when you are."

I turn, grinning, enjoying his toned physique and strong arms. He has a six pack that could be on the cover of an exercise magazine. "I'm ready."

When life's so great, it's hard to believe - enjoy it.

"How are you inside already?" I ask, dipping a toe into the peach-scented bubble-filled waters and wincing.

"Brute force." Landon smirks.

"It's going to take me a minute," I say, shedding the robe and trying to dip my toe a bit further in.

It is way, way, way hot. Though I'm sure once my body is more used to the temperature, I'll love it.

"Don't rush," Landon says easily, his hazel eyes steady on my bare curves.

"Perv," I tease, splashing him.

"Careful." He splashes me back and I squeal.

"Come and get me," he shoots back.

And - screw it - I do. I throw myself in, wincing at the insane scalding heat ripping through me, but it's worth it to see the look on his face as I wrap my arms around him and press my lips to his: shock, delight, arousal.

The kiss, of course, makes any lingering burning from the water fall away.

By the time we separate, the water is just the right temperature. Landon wraps his arms around me. "Hey."

"Hey."

"I like kissing you."

"What a coincidence." I giggle. God, I'd seem like a complete idiot to anyone watching. But I don't care. I'm happy, stupidly, crazily happy. "I like kissing you too."

"Good." Landon's lips land on mine. "Because these lips aren't going anywhere."

We kiss and we kiss and we kiss. Our tongues entwine. We kiss each other's necks and ears. Our hands explore each other's bodies.

His cock is hard, and it only makes sense, me sitting on him, for it to slip inside.

Oh... fuck.

Pleasure explodes through me.

Our eyes lock.

"Oh yeah?" I say, breathless already.

"Fuck yeah," he says, flexing inside me.

I ride him. Swaying my hips side to side, I grind onto him nice and deep. It feels so, so good.

His pleased grunts are hot as hell too. He grips my hips, eyes half-lidded with pleasure. "Kyra. Fucking Kyra. You're... fuck... I can't get enough of you."

I start riding him even harder. His face twists. "You're... fucking amazing. Don't stop, baby. You're fucking amazing. The best. I... you... yes..."

My own moans drown out the rest of what he was saying. I'm there. Almost there. Oh. Fuck. Yes.

All at once, I'm not at the summit, I'm over it, peaking all over him - "Yes, and yes, and yes!"

He slaps my ass, slapping the rest of it out of me, the orgasm I didn't even realize I was still holding inside me. "Yes!"

And still, after, I still have more in me. I ride him harder, and his face tenses once again with pleasure. "How do you... Fuck, Kyra. Fucking sexiest... best... I love you. I fucking love you."

And as our eyes bore into each other, as the shock of his words tumbles around my head, as I come on him and he comes inside of me, all I can think is that there's nothing in this world that's ever felt as right as this.

**

I awake to something hard against my ass. Something I want.

Even half-asleep as I am, my body knows what it wants. I nuzzle my ass against his cock and it slips right inside my pussy.

Whoa. Yeah.

At first, just shallowly, he teases my pussy. In and out. A bit in, then out. Fuck.

I'm already so wet.

I shove myself back onto him, so that he's in me deeper, better, more. He grunts. I moan.

This, this is what I need. This is what makes sense of everything else.

Fuck logic and sense and 'should' - this is what decides things.

Landon wraps his arms around me and pulls me to him. In and out, deep and deeper. Our bodies slap together and he caresses my breasts, my ass. We're one movement, one forward motion. One undeniable urge satisfying itself. Yes. Fucking yes.

"That's it," Landon murmurs into my ear, "That's my girl."

And it's just like before, only not. It's even better.

He runs his hands along my curves like worship. He moves me around, angles my torso and legs like I'm a doll. Although nothing gets him jackhammering me harder than hearing my moans pick up.

"You gonna come for me, baby?" he says, when my body breaks into uncontrollable shaking, with my legs propped up against his chest, as he drills me nice and deep. "You gonna say my name?"

Everything is a groan, pleasure climbing higher and higher, until he pauses. "You gonna say my name when you come?"

"Fuck you," I moan, twisting myself onto him.

I'm so close, I just need...

"Fuck you," he growls back.

And then he plows me harder than ever, and everything blasts away. Yes, yes, yes!

"Landon!" a voice that's not mine cries out.

"Kyra!" a voice that's not his returns.

And all I can think, silly in his arms as our bodies wrap around each other and then pick up where we left off, more of more, more pleasure, more us, is that this is like a fairytale.

That this - us - we work. I was wrong about everything, too afraid. This - us - we work.

And then, as Landon's hard cock goes inside me again, it all starts up again.

**

Morning.

I'm warmer than usual and... naked?

My eyes snap open and I remember. Ohhh... Fuck.

Ohhh fuck no.

I swallow, then strain around to peer at Landon's peaceful still-asleep face.

Oh fuck yes?

I mean, the sex was... ugh.

I put that aside. Better not think about it. For now. Or a while.

I sink back into the bed, closing my eyes.

Maybe if I could sleep for just a little longer...

My eyes snap open.

So much for going slow. How was this past night in any way, shape or form 'slow'?

Still, am I really sorry it happened? The grocery shopping, the PJ shopping, the dinner, the dancing, the hotel room, the Jacuzzi, the sex, Landon saying "I love you..."

Hold the hell up.

Did Landon actually say "I love you?"

It doesn't matter. It's not the time to think of that - or be here.

It's time to go.

I take longer than strictly necessary to extricate myself from his arms. The last thing I need right now is him waking up. This is taking all of my self-control as it is, even with the persistent voice banging on the inside of my skull: What the hell have you done?

It scrambles me into my clothes, proper buttons to proper button holes be damned. Shoes without socks, dress on the dresser. And then, one last look at him.

God, that beautiful, beautiful man. He looks so peaceful, so content. As if I'm still in his arms.

Although, who knows, maybe he's just a peaceful-looking sleeper in general?

I pause. Nope, can't remember.

But still, am I really going to leave like this without saying goodbye?

My phone goes off. I don't check it, but I remember. The real reason I have to go, can't spend the rest of the day and the day after that with him.

I have a daughter. A life.

Luckily, there's no one to see my walk of shame (is it a walk of shame?) as I leave the hotel. I get to admire the mirror-panel walls, the marble step that leads to every room.

Yes, everyone's busy living their lives, minding their own business. I need to get back to doing the same. I was doing well. So very well, before.

I walk to my car as fast as I can walk while still walking. I get inside. Sit down.

Stare at the empty Volvo parked in the space in front of me.

What. The. Fuck.

Before the answer to that can land, I start up my car, get driving.

There's no room for me to sit here and process this how I need. Maybe I'll never process it. Maybe some things can never be processed.

Maybe there's no easy answer to falling for a guy who broke your heart already, and figuring out how to trust him again, and wondering if the feeling in your gut that it's wrong is knowledge or fear. God, and I still haven't told him.

Right now, though, I'm on my way to pick my daughter up from Mom's. That's the only thing that matters. That's important. That I have room for.

So, I drive the speed limit, stop at stop lights, and am very careful to not let myself think about what I've done.

As soon as Mom's powder-blue front door opens, Madison bobs up, halfway through tying her shoes, races to give me a great big bear hug. "Mom!"

She's got her hair in scraggly pigtails I can tell will be a job untangling tonight. Mom always was hilariously bad at doing hair.

Seeing her, it suddenly wells up in me.

God, my daughter - my beautiful, wonderful daughter.

"What's the matter, Mommy?" she says.

It's then that I realize I've been so caught up in myself that I haven't been hugging her back.

As I wrap my arms around her and hold her tight, it occurs to me, what I can't say: Mommy's keeping a secret, and it's wrong.

CHAPTER 13

Landon

What.

My eyes snap open. I don't remember falling asleep here.

I yawn, prop myself up partway. My gaze lands on the empty but ruffled other side of the bed.

OK, now I remember. But where's Kyra?

The door to the bathroom is open. Her dress is neatly folded on the white wooden dresser.

Gone?

I check my phone.

Nothing. Huh.

I get myself out of bed and take a shower. Even though the water pressure is just right, I don't stay in long.

As I brush my teeth, my reflection's wearing a scowl.

Something is up. Maybe.

After the Jacuzzi and wine - did I really drink three-quarters of the bottle? - my memory goes fuzzy.

At any rate, when I call her, she doesn't pick up. I get up and get going. I'm not about to sit around here moping about it.

I pack away my stuff, then get home.

Traffic's shitty and the radio is all sappy pop that makes me want to punch the steering wheel. Some punk would go nicely with my mood.

Back at my place, Nolan is waiting at my dinner table, somehow sprawled on two chairs. "Call me crazy, but I've heard a rumor."

"Not in the mood," I tell him.

I only feel like hitting the gym, really.

"Neither am I, honestly." Nolan chomps on some popcorn as he glares at me. "But when the one ex I actually have good rapport with calls me to tell me that she's seen you riding high with some girl who sounds suspiciously like our Kyra, then my brother card comes into play."

I open the fridge. No-thing. The sink has a mind-boggling number of dirty dishes piled in it, though. Jesus, how many dishes can one person create in a few hours? Then again, this is Nolan.

"Not a big deal," I mutter.

He rises, still popcorn-chomping away. "Why not tell me, then?"

"Because it isn't."

"Bullshit. You're getting involved again."

"What difference does it make?"

"What difference it makes is that this woman is employed by a company that is hell-bent on burning us to the ground. If they succeed, our company, our livelihoods are toast."

"Cool it," I tell him, "It's not about that with her."

"No?" He quirks an eyebrow. "You've never mentioned Dad when you two have been together?"

"He's come up, but it's not like that. She's not with me to fish for information."

"Maybe not. Still, you're being really fucking stupid. This girl almost messed up things for you one time - you gonna let her do it again?"

I spin around to glare at him. "That was on me, not her, and you know it."

"All I know is that you fucked up everything all those years ago. Just don't want you to go down that road again."

"Drop it, Nolan."

"No. You're being stupid. You know you are."

"Fuck off."

"Fine." He marches for the door, taking the bag of popcorn with him. "But don't say I didn't warn you. That woman is bad fucking news. How much do you even know about her, this time around?"

"Enough. What is that supposed to mean, anyway?"

"Nothing." He opens the door, waves. "Just that you're being a selfish prick. Have a nice day."

"You too," I yell after him, but he's already slammed the door behind him.

I sit there for a long time, glaring at the door.

Fucking Nolan. What the fuck does he know?

I go to the microwave and make myself a bag of popcorn too.

**

Monday comes, and there's another court date.

She strides into the courtroom with a black suit dress that gives me an instant erection. Her hard gaze and sure smile give no sign of what she did over the rest of the weekend. All she told me when I texted was: Sorry, busy.

If I have anything to say about it, she'll be busy tonight.

Over the next couple of hours, Kyra goes on to thrash us in court. Dirk does his part defending us valiantly, but it doesn't help that Goldtree actually has a decent case. Plus, they've got evidence that Collin met up with a Goldtree executive at the fundraiser for the new children's hospital a year and a half back, the one I remember him trying to make me go to. I didn't. Who knows what would've happened if I had? Would we still be dealing with this?

At any rate, you can't argue with photos. Although it still isn't an open-and-shut win for Goldtree, either. Just because Dad talked with that executive doesn't mean he plagiarized from them.

Seeing Kyra up on the stand, verbally eviscerating us, in her fucking element is just... shit. Acting as if there's nothing between us. It's infuriating. Arousing.

On our way out, I stop her in the lobby. "Aren't you forgetting something?"

She eyes me uncomprehendingly, that same confident veneer on that I want to rip off.

"Picnic with me - tonight," I tell her.

"I can't."

"Why not?"

"I have plans."

"Now, then. I've got everything in a cooler in my car already."

She eyes me curiously. "You planned this too?"

This was not how this conversation was supposed to go.

"C'mon," I say, "you can do an hour. The hearing ended early."

She bites her lip. I'm right, and she knows it.

I lean in so that my lips brush her ear. "Don't make me make a scene. Kiss you how I want to. Right here. Right now."

She pulls away, face flushed, hissing, "Don't you dare."

I step in. "Kyra. Come on. An hour."

"Fine," she says, smoothing her skirt and looking around. No one's seen or noticed anything, though. "An hour. But we're leaving separately and meeting at the Starbucks on the corner."

"Stealth mode." I grin. "Got it."

I'm willing to accept it... for now.

In the Starbucks parking lot, we park side by side. She rolls down her window. I roll down mine.

"I don't know about this," she says.

"Neither do I," I say. "Think we should pick up some brie too? I've only got cheddar."

Her glare just makes me smile. "Seriously."

"I am being serious," I continue. "Wasn't brie your favorite type of cheese?"

"Ugh." She gets out of her car, slamming the door behind her. "There's no winning with you."

If I have any say, we'll both be winning tonight.

"Do I get to know where we're going?" Kyra asks as she gets into my car.

"No," I say.

"Landon."

"A park."

"Fine."

"Good."

I drive a bit.

"You were great today, by the way," I say.

A pause. "You're not mad?"

"No. Why would I be? You're just doing your job."

"I know, this is all just... weird."

"Lucky, too."

Her smiles brightens the car. "I guess."

"I know."

I park on the side of the road, then help her out.

The weight of the cooler as I heft it out reminds me I'm overdue at the gym. I've fallen off a bit since I started seeing Kyra more.

A few minutes later, we're there. Teardrop Park.

"I like the name," Kyra says with a giggle.

"I've yet to see an actual teardrop here," I reply, "but who knows."

She giggles and my face slackens into a dopey smile. Hell, I get stupid around her.

It isn't hard finding a bare patch of grass shaded by some shrubs. I set out the blanket, we sit down and get eating.

"Do I get to know these pressing evening plans?" I ask, as we start on the baguette and cheese.

"No," she says.

"OK."

We eat in silence. There's no one around except an overeager wasp.

"What is it?" I ask.

"What are we doing, Landon?"

"We're having a picnic."

"No, I mean - we're on opposing sides in this big court case, we broke up over nine years ago - what are we doing?" She looks almost angry as she says it.

"Enjoying each other's company."

A bitter laugh.

"What do you want me to say?" I find myself growling, with more anger than intended. "All I know is I like spending time with you. I want to keep doing it. What's so wrong with that?"

"What's so wrong is that I'm not the same girl you were dating nine years ago," she returns, just as angrily. "Things are different now, I'm different, and - there's things you don't know about me."

"Then tell me!"

"It's not that simple!"

Now we're yelling, and all I want to do is kiss her. Kiss away the rage that's arced her eyes into slits.

I do.

She pulls away. "You can't just fix everything with that."

Another kiss. "No?"

She pulls away. "I mean it, Landon. I don't know if I can do this."

"What are you saying?"

She puts down the baguette she's accidentally crumbled in her hand. "I'm saying that this is all messed up. You. Me. Us. I swore I'd never get involved with you again, and now, here I am, having a freaking picnic with you, and - "

I take her hand, squeeze it gently. "Hey."

She's looking away, almost as if she can't bear to look at me. "I don't think I hate you anymore."

A surprised laugh bursts out of me. "That's what this is all about?"

"No, of course not! Just - there's a lot at stake for me here."

"And there isn't for me?"

Now, she's looking at the ground. Even in her severe yet sexy lawyer suit, her hair pulled back into a bun, she's almost painfully gorgeous. I just want to pick her up in my arms, run my hand along her hair, kiss her forehead. Make it better.

But she doesn't want that now.

"What are we doing, Landon?" she asks quietly, finally looking at me. The look she gives me is so sad I'm the one who has to look away.

"I don't care if this doesn't make sense," I find myself saying. "I don't care. OK?"

"OK," she says dully.

"I want to see you. Do you want to see me?"

"It isn't that simple."

"Yes, it is." I turn her chin to face me. "Do you?"

"Yes, of course." A sad smile. "But Landon - "

A finger to her lips. "No buts. Let's just enjoy this picnic, and I'll keep doing a good job not ripping that sexy little suit of yours off in public."

She gives me a playful smack. "Perv."

"You like it."

She laughs. "Just pass me the strawberries."

Too fast, we eat through the baguette and cheese and strawberries. Even the big bar of dark Swiss chocolate we devour in no time.

Talk is easy, light. My mouth is sore from grinning too much.

The sun's come out from the clouds. The rays only serve to illuminate her porcelain skin. That slight honey tint of her eyes. She's so pretty when she smiles.

"So, about tonight," I begin.

"No dice."

"You didn't even hear what I was going to say." Her playing hard to get is getting old.

"Landon."

"Kyra."

"I meant what I said. I'm busy." She checks her phone. "I should be going now, actually."

"Sure."

That phone again. Who knows what the fuck is up.

We get packed up quickly enough. I don't answer the question I want to until we're in my car and I'm driving us back: "Why can't you tell me what you're doing tonight?"

"Why do I have to?"

"You don't have to." I frown. This isn't how I wanted this to go. "Just - I don't see why it's a big secret."

"It's not. I'm just not telling you."

"Isn't that the definition of a secret?"

A sigh. She shakes her head. "I'm not getting into this with you."

"Then don't."

"Good."

"Great."

She turns to face the window. Fuck.

"I didn't want today to end like this," I say.

"Neither did I. You brought it up, though."

"Is it so wrong that I'm curious about you?"

"No." A pause. "Demanding to know what I'm up to isn't being curious, though."

"You're the one who said there's so many things I don't know about you, and then you won't even tell me your slightest plans for tonight."

"Alright." She rounds on me, eyes flashing. Once again, I'm right and she knows it. "Tonight, I have a nice bowl of Moroccan stew I'm going to eat. OK. Happy?"

"I got passed over for stew?"

"Ugh! There's no winning with you."

"You already said that today."

"Guess this is the second time, then."

She turns to the window again.

I'm glaring at the road, the stupid slow drivers. This drive is fucked. This afternoon is. This day is.

I need to get home, do some push-ups. Better yet, go to the gym and lift some weights.

Maybe Nolan is right: I'm letting Kyra too far into my head.

But as for this, I don't think I'm wrong either. Something is up with Kyra. Of course it's up to her whether to tell me. But if she isn't going to, she shouldn't go down the 'there's so many things you don't know about me' path. It's just shitty.

She puts her hand on mine. "Sorry. Guess I'm still in lawyer mode."

"I am too. I don't mean to pry. Not my place."

"It's fine. You were right about me being a hypocrite."

"I said that?"

A chuckle. "Not exactly. But I have been. Saying that you don't know me - and then not letting you. I just - " Her face crumples. "I'm just not ready, I don't think."

"Hey, it's fine." I open my hand so her fingers can thread down through mine.

"It's not, though." At a red light, a glance over finds her face with that same sadness. It takes me a second to get what else is there. Hopelessness.

Maybe I'm just tired and seeing things. What the fuck do I know about what Kyra's thinking or feeling?

"OK, it's not," I say, trying a jokey tone.

An exasperated chuckle. "You don't understand."

"Nope." I pull up to the Starbucks and park back next to her car. Turn off the car. Turn to her, and take both her hands in mine. "But I'm willing to wait on you, Kyra. Give you a chance - if you will for me."

Too long passes after my statement. Happiness mingles with the sadness in those beautiful brown eyes of hers.

CHAPTER 14

Kyra

I lean in to give him a light kiss on the lips, although inside I'm already pulling away. Have to.

"Thank you, Landon," I say.

"Goodbye," I say.

Before he can respond, before I cave and look at him, I walk out, away.

I drive off.

Jesus, that was close. Too close.

Close to what, though?

It seems like all I'm doing lately is driving and trying not to think of my problems. Problem, rather.

Mainly: How can I keep seeing Landon, when it's impossible?

Goldtree could fire me just from the rumor. And then there's Madison. Plus, how Landon never really explained that break-up.

My windshield's blurred. It's started to rain, a haphazard spit.

I turn on the windshield wipers. Stopped at a red, I watch them - back and forth, back and forth, back and forth.

Like me on the whole Landon issue: stay away, bounce back, stay away, bounce back.

How did I let things get this far?

The question hangs until I pick up Madison. Her happy face and purple tutu fill the car as she bounces in. "Mom, when you see our recital you are going to flip!"

I grin at her. "I'm sure, honey."

We're sitting at another red, when, out of nowhere, she says, "Mom, what happened to Dad?"

"What?"

Madison's smile is guilty. "Sorry, I just... you never talk about him."

"You know I don't like to."

"Yeah, but... was he nice?"

"Yeah, he was. But he's gone now, and he's not coming back. I'm sorry."

Recycled comments for a long untouched topic. But it's all I've got.

"Do you... think he'd like me?" Maddy asks tentatively. "If he met me, I mean?"

I take one sad look at her. "Honey, I'm sure of it."

That night, we watch a few episodes of Pinky and the Brain, make glittery paper crowns.

I sit on the couch while she's brushing her teeth, staring into the electric fireplace and its blue-tinged flames.

This needs to stop. Either I tell Landon about Madison or...

There is no 'or'. I have to tell him.

And one day, maybe, I can tell Madison the full, terrible story about her dad. Right now, it's too much for a nine-year-old to swallow. Soon, though.

After I've tucked Madison into bed, she snuggles up to her donut unicorn stuffy, a sleepy smile on her face. "Love you, Mom."

"Love you, Maddy."

Those little upturned lashes, slightly plump rosy cheeks. My little girl. My daughter.

How could I have ever kept her a secret - the best part of me?

There's no answer that brings anything other than guilt, so I leave the room. Now's as good a time as any to finally call Pamela back.

"Hello stranger," she says. "Remember me? Your best friend?"

"I'm sorry," I say. "I've just been busy. Was back at court today."

"Come on, I'm not an idiot," she says gaily. "You've been seeing him."

I sigh. "Guilty as charged. Maybe not for much longer, though."

"What do you mean?"

"It's just messing with my head! And I still haven't told him about Madison."

Silence.

"Pompom?"

"It's just... I get it. It's a big deal. A hugely big deal."

"I keep feeling like I'm lying to him, not telling him. And like I'm betraying Maddy too. What kind of mother keeps her child a secret?"

"The kind who's trying to protect them," she says firmly. "Honestly Ky, don't beat yourself up about it."

"But I do need to tell him."

"Yeah. You do."

"I just keep thinking... this probably can't work anyway, with the case, and how he hurt me before. I don't know, it seems like it'd be easier to just end things without telling him."

"Easier or less scary?"

"Both. I can't afford to mess up my job. And if I tell him about Maddy..."

"But there must be something holding you to him," Pamela says. "You wouldn't have given him a second chance for nothing."

"Something?" I laugh hoarsely. "How about ten somethings? How persistent he's been, how considerate. The dates he's taken me on - yeah, last night we went to the Baccarat Hotel, penthouse suite with a private Jacuzzi... and then, of course, all the parts of him I fell in love with last time. Jesus, sometimes it's like the past years haven't even happened."

"But they did."

"Yeah," I say, "They did. And I can't stop thinking: if he dumped me once, with no real explanation or reason, what's to stop him from doing it again?"

"Have you asked him?" Pamela says. "I mean, really told him how much it has been bugging you, not knowing?"

"Not really," I admit. "There's just so many things about us being together that are messed up right now."

"Then pick one and fix it," Pamela says. "Or dump him. As you said, that's probably the easier option."

I sigh. "And the smartest. Yet here I am."

"Hey, you'll figure it out. Remember, you figured out getting through law school as a single mom."

"True." I smile. "Thanks." It comes to me in a rush: I miss my friend. "Want to come over tonight or tomorrow?"

"Wednesday. I've got a hot date with the tax man tonight."

"Pamela."

"I'm not kidding. Taxes are literally due tomorrow, and the tax man - accountant guy - has a shit-ton of questions for me. Apparently, I've been, ahem, a bit liberal with my business spending."

I chuckle. "Didn't you try to write off a manicure since it brought you 'inner spiritual peace'?"

"Come on!" Pamela says indignantly. "It's important for my mental health to look presentable. Plus, if I don't look my best, how can I be expected to perform my best?"

I just laugh. "Good luck."

"Yeah, yeah, I should go. I need to find a bunch of receipts, too. You have a good night, though. And don't worry. Landon might take you telling him better than you think."

"I hope so. Night, Pamela."

"Night, Kyra."

I go in to check on Madison with a small smile.

Just like that, I've made up my mind. I'm going to tell him. Not now, through a text or a call, even though I'm burning to. In person.

No more putting it off. It's time.

**

Next morning, after I've gotten Maddy to school, I call him up.

"Hey, I was thinking about you," he says. "What are your thoughts on hot pink shirts?"

"Uh... they're OK?"

"For me, I mean. I'm at the store."

I grin, imagining Landon in hot pink - hot, as usual. I guess double hot in the pink. Hehe.

Yep, I'm in silly mode with him on my mind.

"Go for it."

"Cool. What about you - just calling to talk?"

"Not exactly. I was thinking we could go out tonight. You heard of the Marbarow Fair?"

"Think so - edge of town, right? I'm game. I'll pick you up?"

"I'd rather us meet there."

"You're never gonna show me your place, are you?" I can hear the smile in his voice.

"Not yet."

"Challenge accepted - see you tonight."

"See you," I say, bouncing on my toes.

Tonight it is. I'm really doing this.

The rest of the day passes way too fast. I get some work done, talk to a potential client. Shoot some emails back and forth with some Goldtree employees who are planning on testifying.

Before I know it, we're meeting in the parking lot. Landon was already there when I arrived.

"I was worried I was going to be late, so I came early," he explains with a smile.

I chuckle. "Make sense."

"I got us tickets."

"Landon!"

"What?" A wink. "I thought that's why you invited me here."

"No, I invited you here because I thought you'd wear your hot pink shirt," I joke, eyeing him and his black t-shirt that shows off his strong arms. Shit, focus, Kyra. "But no go, clearly."

We crack up, and Landon loops his arm in mine. "C'mon. We have a merry-go-round to go to. Did I ever tell you about how we rode it once when we were little and Emerson cried and shrieked so much that they actually stopped the ride to haul him off?"

I chuckle. "Nope. How are they anyway, your brothers? I feel like a jerk for not asking earlier."

"Oh, they're good," he says lightly.

Just good?

It could be that he feels weird mentioning them, since we used to all hang out from time to time, and now... yeah, nothing. It makes sense, though. This thing we're in, whatever it is, it's still an unknown. Plus, it's not like I've been introducing him to my family or friends left, right and center, either.

Although it would show me that all this isn't just talk. Not that I think it is. Agh.

Inside the park, we walk past the game stalls, all bright flashing lights and colorful prizes. Landon pauses at one when he sees me eyeing its cute prize hats.

"Landon," I say.

"Kyra," he says.

"You don't have to - " Before the words are halfway out of my mouth, Landon has already walked up and handed the employee a ticket. It's a strongman game with a giant colorful tower counting up to 240.

"Here goes," he says, a determined set to his jaw.

He lifts the hammer and slams it down, face contorted with effort.

The weight shoots up... 150... 200... and - celebratory music, flashing lights - 240!

"Whoa!" the employee says. Her ponytail bobs as she gestures to the hat stand beside. "Take your pick."

A minute or so later, I'm walking away with a brand-new black suede hat on my head.

"Hold up," Landon says.

I pause as he peers at me and smiles. "You make that hat look damn good."

I chuckle, putting it on his head. "You don't look so bad yourself."

Landon snorts, trying - and failing - to mash it onto his head. "Head's too big."

"Head's just right," I reply.

A smile that melts me as he places the hat back on my head. "If you say so..."

He steals a kiss. Then another. My arms slide around him, into his jean pockets. We're in the middle of a fair, and I feel at home.

Tell him. Tell him now.

I sigh. I should tell him - of course I should. But not right now. Not yet. Soon.

"Which ride first?" Landon asks, hand entwining mine.

"Whatever's closest?" I look around, but all I see nearby are more fair games.

"Any must-do's?" Landon asks.

"Ferris wheel, definitely. You?"

"I think I see the swings nearby. You game?" He squeezes my hand.

I squeeze his hand. "I'm game."

Before we get there, Landon insists on getting us some corn dogs. And ice cream. And a t-shirt with our faces on it. When he's about to get waylaid by a photo booth, I stop him.

"We're never going to get on any rides at this rate."

Landon rakes a hand through his light brown hair, his generous lips in a pout. "Shit. Got sidetracked. Sorry."

"Don't apologize" - I tug him towards the swings - "just take me on a ride."

Minutes later, we're on it, side by side, our held hands breaking free. The wind whips at us softly, and I have to hold my hat in my lap to keep it from blowing away. I look over to see Landon trying not to grin.

"What? I ask.

"Nolan always said swings are for wusses," he admits, a bit ruefully.

"Screw Nolan."

He laughs. "Screw him."

"This is fun," I say.

"This is what it feels like being with you."

And I just look at him and laugh and smile because it's true.

It occurs to me then, high up in the air, as the odd waft of popcorn and cotton candy and Landon's tempting scent hits me, that I'm happy. Stupidly so.

Even with what's coming, what I have to do, at least there's now. At least there's us.

Next is the merry-go-round. We try getting on the same horse, but the ride employee isn't having it, so we settle on two horses side by side. Mine has a whipping pink mane and frenzied eyes, while his aquamarine one looks like it's enjoying a nice bubble bath.

The peppy waltz begins and our horses start bobbing up and down, on different tracks.

"Tell me about the time Emerson got kicked off," I tell him. "Why was he so scared?"

"Nolan told him the horses were possessed and that, every year, they killed one kid that they didn't like to take his cotton candy. Emerson gave him his cotton candy, but he was still freaked. Greyson and I tried reassuring him, but it didn't work."

I laugh. "So, Nolan was always a dick, basically?"

"In some ways." His mouth quirks. "But he is my twin. Besides, I haven't always been great myself."

"That's one way of putting it."

"Listen," he says, "I am sorry. For everything I put you through."

"It's OK," I say.

Luckily, the ride has stopped, so I have an excuse to get off my horse and away. Because really, I'm not sure I want to admit the next part to him: that I appreciate him apologizing, but that doesn't mean I can fully trust him. I'm not sure I can afford to, after what he pulled all those years ago.

Plus, there's that persistent voice in my head: Tell him.

And my ducking, not-good-enough answer: Not now. Not yet.

As we leave the ride by the exit gate, the ride employee scows at us from her phone. There are virtually no other riders, and we clearly interrupted whatever game she's been playing. Unperturbed, Landon says, "Let's go horseback riding sometime."

"But I thought - "

"Yeah, still not a big horse guy. That whole horse-kicked-me-when-I-was-five thing. I don't know. Maybe it's worth a shot. It sure looked fun back when you boarded... what was her name?"

"Spirit," I remind him with a half-smile, "After the movie."

"Oh yeah, I remember now. God, you loved that horse. What happened to her?"

"Life happened. I got my degree, my job. Got busy."

And had a kid - tell him!

Not yet.

If you keep putting it off...

"Anything up?" he asks, "You seem a bit..."

That's your cue.

"I haven't been sleeping great lately."

That's true, at least. Late at night is when my mind likes to run through the unsolvable dilemmas of my life - mainly the whole 'Landon but work' thing.

His arms wrap around me, press me to him. "Maybe you need some company."

God, what those arms do to me...

I sink into them, let my eyes close. Let myself imagine that everything really is how it feels - safe, perfect.

Tell him.

"Next ride?" I ask, pulling free.

"If you say so."

On the way, he gets us the biggest cotton candy I've ever seen.

"Is this a good idea?" I ask as we sit on a bench and start eating.

He just laughs. "Too late."

Next thing I know, he's lifted some cotton candy to my mouth. I eat it, my mouth brushing his fingers.

Fuck. Nothing about him can be tame, can it?

Now I'm feeding him, and he's feeding me, and our sticky lips are giggle-kissing and...

This time it's Landon who pulls away. "Want to come over?"

At my questioning look, he amends, "My place, I mean."

"What - now?"

His lips press together and his eyebrows dip. "Not that I'm not enjoying myself, but..." A look around to confirm there's no one nearby and he brings my hand to the front of his jeans.

Ah yes. Now I understand.

"Not my problem you're hard," I murmur with a saucy smirk.

He crosses his arms across his chest. "You're not going to take responsibility?"

"OK, maybe a bit. But you'll just have to wait."

Will he? What about telling him?

Stretching out his powerful arms, Landon sets off, taking my hand. "Let's get going, then. Less kissing, more riding." He winces as I crack up. "Not like that."

"Don't worry," I whisper in his ear as we approach the Ferris wheel. "I'll see what I can do after."

If he even still wants to see me after this.

Getting onto the Ferris wheel, still nibbling away at the hopelessly too-big cotton candy, it all comes crashing down on me.

I can't put it off anymore.

And yet, I can't say it now either - now with my whole body settled in a too-much-shit-food hangover.

Not that I've even perfected what to say. I tried writing it out a bunch of times at home, but all I got was a notebook full of scratched-out nonsense. After all, how do you tell someone: sorry, but I have a daughter that I haven't told you about for weeks? Are there any words on the planet that could soften that, make it palatable?

Is there some sort of strategy that could help? A slow lead-in, or - BAM! - hit him over the head with it?

How should I start?

So, there's something I've been meaning to tell you...

So, you know how I said there's things you don't know about me?

Landon, I'm really sorry, but there's something really important you should know. Someone, rather...

"Here we are," Landon says, breaking me out of my reverie.

Here we are is right. Cool night breeze on all sides. Landon's hand in mind. A toss of murky stars overhead, a toss of lights further out. Rides nearby are the most visible thing, but further out it's harder to see.

Like my and Landon's future - if we have one. If we do, one thing is for certain: I have to tell him. Now.

"Here we are," he says again, more softly this time.

Perfect time for a kiss - so of course he leans in for one.

It would be so easy to let that kiss take over, let it steal this moment. So right.

But I can't. I've put this off long enough.

His lips have just about landed on mine when I pull away. Swallow. Say: "There's something I have to tell you."

His face is disappointed already - a lost kiss - but it's about to get way more disappointed. Or shocked. Or... I don't know.

Stop putting it off. Just say it.

"I..."

Just fucking say it.

"Have a daughter."

It came out a croak and now I can't bear to look at him, but it doesn't matter. It's done.

Still, I can feel him gaping at me, speechless. For ten seconds, thirty, fifty, a minute...

When he does speak, it's an uncertain, "Bad joke, Kyra."

I look at him and see nothing but uneasiness. "I'm not joking."

He searches my face, the frown taking over his entire face. "Kyra... what the hell?"

I don't wait to see it come to his eyes.

"I'm so sorry," I say. "I know it's not at all enough. I should've told you before, weeks ago. Just... I didn't know how, and I wanted to protect her." A tentative smile. "My daughter. Madison."

He's looking away now, past me, disappointment etching all his features. "Madison."

The Ferris wheel has started carrying us down. There's a sick churning in my gut, but it's not from that. The night air seems cooler. The stars have receded out of reach. The only thing I can smell is smoke from somewhere.

How could I ever have thought that this was a good idea? Telling him, him and me in the first place.

"What else aren't you telling me?" he asks quietly.

"What? That's it. I think that's enough." My nervous giggle falls flat.

We're at the bottom now, getting off, leaving by the exit gate.

Landon stops a few steps away. "There's someone else. Isn't there?"

"Yeah, my daughter."

The gaze he cuts me with is merciless. "Not what I meant, and you know it."

"What are you saying?"

Is that it - or is it something else?"

"What are you talking about?"

He's shaking his head, mouth twisted and ugly. "Us coming here in separate cars and having to sneak around... you constantly going to check your phone. There's someone else, isn't there? Someone else who's Madison's father."

I try to touch his shoulder. "Landon - "

He shrugs me off, stalking off a few paces to stop, back tensed. "None of this adds up. If it was really just that you had a daughter, you would've just told me. There has to be something else - someone else."

I gape at him for a few seconds, shocked, before I realize that I waited too long.

"No, no, there isn't, of course there isn't," I protest, "You're not even listening to me - "

"No, I'm using my fucking brain. Something I haven't been doing lately, apparently."

Landon stops, takes a miserable look at me. "You've been using me, Kyra. Killing us in court. Distracting me. Now you want to throw this daughter bomb to end things? Be my guest."

He starts walking, heading for the parking lot. I hurry after him. "That's not what I've been trying to do - "

"Then what has this been to you?" he says, without so much as a glance back. "Wait, I'll answer for you. Clearly, nothing. Clearly, you never saw this going anywhere."

He keeps on heading for the parking lot. I follow after him without a word.

My head's buzzing with all the different things I could say, should say.

Landon, of course there's no one else, I just - Landon, you have to believe me, I never intended to - Landon, please -

But he won't go, leaving things like this between us. He wouldn't dare.

And screw him for believing that, thinking the worst of me. Doesn't he know me better than that? Does he really think I'm capable of doing something like that?

But we get to his car, and I still haven't said a word.

"Don't worry," he says, opening his car door. "I don't see this going anywhere anymore either."

He won't leave it just like that -

He gets in the car and closes the door.

He's not going to just drive off like this -

He starts up the car.

I know Landon, he wouldn't just leave things like -

He drives away.

How is this happening?

I stand there long enough for it to get weird, if anyone else was around. But it's just me.

Funny. With all the worst-case scenarios I played out in my head, I never thought of this one.

CHAPTER 15

Landon

Adrenaline is thrumming through my veins. God, a kid. A goddamn kid. Whose?

Is he still in the picture? What else has she been keeping from me?

How can I believe a goddamn word she tells me now?

"Fuck!" I yell, smacking my palm against the steering wheel.

What the fuck? How could I be so fucking stupid? How the fuck could I let this happen?

And the court case...

This was all a sick game to her. I heard it myself that first day: "I hate you." Why would I think that could change so fucking easily?

Back at home, I sit in my living room in the dark, scroll and scroll and scroll through my phone's contact list. Mostly female names disconnected from any face or feeling. Like reading through the phone book - Taryn, Nancy, Jessica, Celine, Natalie.

I put away my phone.

Why even bother?

I don't owe Kyra any fucking thing. I ought to text one of them - text all of them, one of those mass 'hey's' that used to be Nolan's signature.

But I'm not in the fucking mood. Not to stretch my face into a smile, contort my voice into some sort of lie.

Right now, I need to be alone.

******

Next day, I stalk into the office like a tiger for prey.

It's not hard to find. We're out of half a dozen office supplies, haven't had a team meeting in weeks, and there's a bunch of paperwork I let slide.

How could I have let things slide so completely?

It only takes me a couple of manic, rage-fueled hours to get caught up, though.

I schedule a meeting with Dirk, who's grim but won't throw in the towel yet. Which is good, since that's what we're fucking paying him for.

Back at my office, while I'm sorting through mail - 97% of which is complete garbage - Greyson calls me up. "How are you doing?"

"Fine," I say.

"You busy? I can call back."

"Just doing mail. It's not important."

"You're in a productive mood."

"What can I say, I'm a productive guy." I can't resist adding: "You don't have to worry about the Kyra thing anymore either."

"Ah."

"I'm an idiot," I add.

"You been talking to Nolan?"

"No, but he was right."

"Shit. I'm sorry."

"It's OK. Just pissed I let things get this far."

Silence. I can almost hear the gears turning in Greyson's head. "Got plans tonight?"

"No. Why?"

"Come have dinner with Harley and me. We snagged a table at La Caverna."

"You don't have to do that. I'm not a wreck."

"I want to. Come on, it's been a while."

"I don't know..."

"Up to you." Never did I think there'd be a time I called Greyson 'indefatigably cheerful', but here we are. "But I'm pretty sure Nolan wanted to take you out to O'Malley's, so you could avoid that."

"I'm in," I say immediately.

For whatever reason, Nolan's obsessed with that Irish hovel with horrible food and perpetually bickering though busty waitresses.

Greyson chuckles. "Great. See you at seven."

Sure enough, a few hours later, Nolan calls me up for a 'long-overdue-dinner at a premier establishment', which I have to, unfortunately, decline.

The rest of the day, I continue my fury of productivity. It keeps me from checking my phone too much, seeing as I know already what I'd find there: a grand total of nothing.

Once seven rolls around, I head to the restaurant.

Harley and Greyson are already there in the entry, both dressed to the nines and looking obnoxiously happy.

"Isn't this place cool?" Harley enthuses, her gesture to cavey surroundings making the low lights illuminate her silver dress and jewelry. "Oh, and hey there."

We give each other a light hug.

"How's Dakota doing?" I ask dutifully.

She chuckles. "You don't have to feign interest, you know. I know you and the other brothers are about as interested in kids as you are in starfish. Though I appreciate you asking - he's good. Starting to talk already."

I chuckle too. "Got me. You look great, though."

"Careful now," Greyson says lightly.

"Didn't mean it like that," I return easily.

Harley just grins, then flexes her bicep. "I've taken up this new yoga regimen."

"La Caverna," Greyson says, purposely a bit loud, smiling at the echo his voice makes. "Place is well-named."

"Let's see if the food is good too," Harley says, hooking her arm in his.

I let them go a bit ahead of me, watching them. They make it look so easy. Guess it is when you're with the right one.

Now, as for me and Kyra...

Not thinking about it.

"How are things with you?" Harley asks me after we sit down. "You enjoying being President?"

I shrug. "Not sure enjoying is the word."

"Babe." Greyson takes Harley's hand and squeezes it. "You don't enjoy being President - you bear it."

"Oh." She giggles. "My mistake."

"Should I even ask about the court case?" Greyson asks.

"Better you don't," I say, hands clenched on the edge of the table.

Another one of my fuck-ups. Hopefully not an irrevocable one, though.

Just then, the waitress comes, notepad at the ready, so we order. I'm about to order a bottle of wine when Greyson stops me. "We didn't want to tell anyone, but... Harley's expecting."

"Again?" Cue smile. "Congratulations, you two!"

Harley wrinkles her nose. "I know: again. Guess it'll be nice to get them over with."

She and Greyson crack up.

"It's fine," I tell the waitress, "I'll still take the wine."

I grin at Harley and Greyson. "More for me."

Once the waitress has left, Harley fixes me with a worried smile. "You OK? Greyson told me about..."

"I'm fine."

Greyson squeezes her shoulder lightly. "Told you, babe. Landon probably doesn't want to talk about it."

"What happened, though?" Harley asks, before her hand flies to her mouth. "Oh God, I'm so sorry. That just slipped out. Feel free to tell me to go to hell." A small smile. "Although I am curious."

"She has a kid," I say.

Then, seeing their expressions and realizing how it sounded, I clarify: "She has a kid that she didn't tell me about for weeks. And God only knows what else she's been hiding from me. The kid must have a father, so she probably has a husband or boyfriend in the picture, for all I know. She was just using me to get dirt on Storm Media."

"If she has a husband or boyfriend already, then she's a really shitty partner," Harley says quietly.

"Yeah. Well. Who knows? All I know is that she's been acting weird lately, and that's probably why."

"Fuck her," Greyson says, sipping his water. "You're probably right."

"Am I the only one who thinks maybe she really just has a kid and waited too long to tell you?" Harley wonders aloud.

As we look at her, she continues, "Don't shoot the messenger, but maybe she was just freaked about telling you she has a kid. Wasn't ready for you to meet them yet. It is a big deal."

"But then why not tell him that?" Greyson says reasonably.

"Exactly," I agree.

Harley shrugs. "I can't answer that one for you. But hasn't this whole... relationship been kind of messy from the start?"

"Sorry," she says, seeing my look, "Greyson might've filled me in on a few of the details."

"What?" Greyson says, under my glare. "Sorry, man, but we tell each other everything."

"I'd rather not talk about it," I say finally.

"Fair enough," Harley acquiesces.

The rest of the dinner is more pleasantries, chatting about the Coldplay concert in town next month that they snagged tickets for, how Dakota has a thing for throwing macaroni, how Nolan's new comedy routine is almost too controversial. My mind isn't really in it.

I hardly taste the river salmon I ordered. I drink some Cabernet but it only makes things fuzzy, and not in a good way.

At the end of the night, I go home and sit in the same spot in my living room as before.

I get up, do a few pushups. Sit down.

Get up, put away the dishes. Sit down.

Fuck.

I don't want to think about it. But could Harley have been right?

I get out my phone, glare at it.

Before I know quite what I'm doing, I've called Kyra up. No answer.

Another call - no answer.

Another call - what the fuck am I doing? - no answer.

Another - "Landon, what the hell do you want?"

Oh. Shit.

"To talk," I tell her.

"It's eleven o'clock at night," Kyra grumbles. "I'm about to go to sleep."

"Doesn't have to take long. I just wanted to... is there someone else?"

"How could you even ask me that?" Kyra demands.

All at once, I know. She's telling the truth. She always was.

"So, all the phone and weirdness - that was just because you have a kid," I say.

"Yes. Because I have a daughter. Like I told you."

"Don't act all high and mighty with me," I snap. "You were the one who was ducking around, not telling me for weeks. Acting like someone acts when there's someone else."

"Yeah, there was - my daughter."

"As you keep saying."

"It's not like we even had the exclusive talk anyway," Kyra continues. "So I'd be well within my rights to be seeing someone else. Not that I have been, but still."

"I thought we understood each other. That we were on the same page."

"And what page is that? Because you sure as shit haven't shown it to me."

"Isn't it obvious?" Fuck, she's really making me spell this out for her. "We're trying again."

"OK."

"OK. That's it?"

"I don't know what to say, Landon." Her voice is mad, constrained. "You accused me of using you, cheating on you. You freaked out on me."

"Can you blame me? That was a pretty huge thing to be keeping from me."

"And I'm sorry. But I still can't believe that you'd think I was capable of that. I thought you knew me better than that."

"I did - I do, I just..." Damn, how to explain it? "You've changed a lot. So have I. And that thing you said to me, that first day: I hate you. It made an impression."

"Yeah, well how you dumped me made an impression too."

"Kyra. Are we ever going to get past that?"

"I don't know," she says miserably. "All I know is that it took me a long-ass time to work up to telling you about Madison, and then it blew up in my face."

"I'm sorry for that. I just wish I understood - "

"This whole time, we haven't really known what this was," Kyra argues. "It's been going in fits and starts. I didn't want you meeting her until I knew for sure."

"For sure what?"

"That it's going to work between us."

Does that mean what I think it does? "And you know now?"

"No, I don't. It just didn't feel right not telling you anymore."

"Thanks for that, I guess. Although I still don't see why you couldn't have just told me all that."

"Yeah, I could've," she says wearily. "But I didn't. OK?"

"OK."

"OK."

Silence.

"I should go," she says.

"So, that's it?" I say.

"Landon, you accused me of cheating on you and basically being a terrible, manipulative person. Sorry, I'm not dying to talk to you right now."

"What about later... in a few days?" I ask.

"Your first instinct was to jump to the conclusion that I've been using you and cheating on you."

"Yeah, I made a mistake, we've established that."

"But what we haven't established is what to do about it," she says. "This all has got me thinking..."

Fuck me.

She better not be getting at what I think she is.

CHAPTER 16

Kyra

"I can't do this," I tell him. "I can't be with someone who doesn't trust me."

"Really?" he says. "You're really going to hold my reaction against me? Kyra, you dropped a literal bomb on me last night."

I swallow. He's right. I know he's right. But I also know that I can't do this. I can't be fully honest with him like I want to. I can't get my head around this.

It's just too hard.

"Give me a chance," he says, softly now. "To make it up to you."

A sad laugh. "Do you take anything I say seriously?" I ask.

"Only when it's what I want to hear."

Another sad laugh. "Can't you see how messed up that is?"

"Have I made you do anything you didn't want to?"

"No, but - "

"Case closed. I want to be with you, Kyra. That's the long and the short of it. Daughter, no daughter - strings attached or no strings - I want to be with you. Do you want to be with me?"

God, he makes it sound so easy. "It's not as simple as that - "

"Answer the question," he growls.

"Yes," I snap, "I do."

"Then let me come over. Let me meet your daughter."

"I don't know if I'm ready for that."

"Then let me come over. I don't have to stay the night."

How the hell does he do it? From me being convinced that we can't be together to me thinking that maybe there might be a chance...

I can't stay. I need to go, clear my head.

"I have to go," I tell him.

"Kyra."

"I'm sorry."

"Kyra, please - "

"Goodnight."

I hang up the phone. I turn it off and sink into my couch, staring at nothing.

How is it that doing the right thing doesn't feel right anymore?

**

Getting out of bed the next day is a drag. It's a court day today, and I'm dreading it. How am I supposed to stay clear of Landon when he's at the fucking courthouse, looking sexy as hell in his suit du jour?

Whatever. I'll take this opportunity to rip him a new one. See how much he wants to see me after that.

Getting Madison ready for school this morning isn't a walk in the park either. She decided to brush her own hair with a vengeance, with the result that the wire bristle brush got stuck in her hair.

"Sorry Mom," she says, wincing as I work carefully to untangle the thing.

Shit. Not the best morning for this.

"It's OK," I say. "I'll figure this out in no time."

Although I'm not so sure of that.

"Grandma says you're stressed and not to bother you," she says, with a guilty frown.

"Well, Grandma is overdoing it. I have a big case, but that's it."

Heck, I'm lying to my kid now too?

Then again, I'm not about to bemoan my man troubles to my nine-year-old.

"OK," she says. "Ow!"

I wave the newly freed brush triumphantly. "Sorry, but it's out. You ready to go?"

Madison rubs at her head with a glare. "If I have any hair left, yeah."

Of course Madison still has a ton of hair, and I manage to get her to the school and me to the courthouse just in time.

In court, I manage to rip Storm Media a new one - again. There are so many similarities between Storm and Goldtree's planned TV shows that I've lost count. The judge and jurors can see it too, I can see it on their faces. We're on track to win.

I grin all the way to the car.

There. That'll show him.

If he thought I was going to take it easy just because of this messed-up situation, then he has another think coming.

"Hey there, stranger," a horribly familiar voice says.

"Hey." Don't look his way - don't look his way. "I have to go pick Madison up. Sorry."

I can still feel his hard look on the side of my head. "It's lunchtime."

"Yeah, well..." I trail off. I've got nothing and he knows it. Now, I dare glare his way. "How about no because I don't want to?"

"That would be fair." God, he's handsome. This time he's skipped the suit for a fitted blue polo that shows off his powerful shoulders, plus black jeans and a devil-may-care smirk that knows I'm wavering and, stupidly and totally randomly, want to kiss him. "Although it would be a lie."

I tear my gaze away. "Landon. Please."

"Have lunch with me."

Just like that. So easy. So assumed. Like - why not? Why not brush your teeth? Why not kiss me and lose every thought in your head?

I exhale. "You never give up. Do you?"

"Nope." He's smiling. Determined. Relaxed. Knows he's got this.

Back in the courtroom may be my playing field, but outside...

"Fine. But we're going to Bentley's down the street," I say, closing the car door and setting off at a quick stride. "Walking. I'm not getting in your car here."

"Stealth mode works for me." He pulls up the collar of his shirt with a wink. "I won't even take your hand until we cross the street."

"You gentleman you." God, this feels so easy. Sliding back into things - no, that's not what's happening. Is it? "Although this doesn't mean - "

"That we're still a thing?" Landon shrugs. "Sure. Have it your way. Call it what you want. As long as I get to see you."

"Just" - a fed-up sigh - "I still haven't decided if I am still seeing you."

"We're seeing each other now." His smile is cheerful enough for the both of us.

"OK, OK," he says, seeing my expression. "I know when to cool it when I'm ahead."

"You're not ahead," I state.

He's definitely ahead, I think.

Bentley's is nice and empty, except for a fresh pancake aroma that gets my stomach growling in anticipation. The red full-size jukebox is playing a Fleetwood Mac song.

The roomy red-seat booth at the back has our name on it. It's got a nice window opening on a sparse hedge that does a not-great job of obscuring the busy road beyond. Landon insists on sitting beside me instead of across from me.

"Weirdo," I mutter.

His grin says it all. "Don't pretend you don't like it."

His leg against mine, his face kiss-close, how could I not like it? How am I supposed to keep my head, though?

I swallow, grabbing the menu to take a look.

Maybe with a bit of food in me...

"So, in there," he says, looking at the menu too. "You killed it."

"Good," I say simply. "Just doing my job."

"Don't I know it. Still, it's a bit of a surprise - the girl who used to shy away from any sort of conflict."

I put the menu down and look at him. "I'm not the girl you dated all those years ago, Landon."

"Yeah, I know. I'm not that guy, either."

I can't stop the smile from touching my face. "We'll see about that."

Under the table, his foot taps mine.

Thank God - there's the waitress. I wave her down. "Sorry, we're kind of in a rush - could I order now?"

"Sure thing, hon," she says, producing a pad of paper from her apron. "What can I get ya?"

"The breakfast special, please. Brown toast. Scrambled eggs. And bacon."

She bobs her head. "Sounds good."

After Landon's ordered and the waitress has left, he eyes me. "In a rush, eh?"

"Do we have to spend all of today fighting?"

He frowns. "I thought you liked it. It is your job."

"I'm just tired of..." I trail off.

"Go on."

"My brain going gummy when I'm around you. There." I glare at him. "Happy now that I said it?"

He sure looks happy. "Thought I was the only one."

"Yeah, well. It's not great when I'm supposed to be suing you. And have a kid to worry about. Today I was so frazzled I almost packed her the salt and pepper shakers for lunch."

Landon cracks up, but soon sobers. "So. About that - what's she like? Madison."

"If you feel comfortable telling me about her," he adds quickly.

"Well, she's... just amazing." Not the word, but it'll do. How am I supposed to do justice to the coolest kid on Planet Earth? "Top of her class in reading, devours every single book and magazine in the house, even got halfway through War and Peace before I realized what she was doing. I guess I'm biased, but she's turned out way better than I would've even hoped. Always in a good mood. She's the best of me. You'll see."

I freeze. How the hell did that last part slip out?

Landon's eyeing me carefully. "Will I? You sure?"

"No," I say quickly, then, "Sorry."

"Don't be." Landon sips his water, his face guarded, though his blue eyes give away his disappointment. "You're just trying to protect her."

I shoot him a thankful smile. "Thanks for being so understanding."

His smile is lopsided but true. "Thanks for coming. I didn't relish a lunch with Nolan. He's been badgering me for days."

"You're avoiding him?"

"He..." Landon makes a face. "Doesn't agree with some of my choices lately. And is making no secret of the fact."

"Oh. You mean me."

Just then, the waitress arrives with our food. We start eating. The scrambled eggs are done to perfection, but I can't let it drop.

"Landon?"

"He's just trying to look out for me," Landon says, dipping the corner of his toast into his poached eggs. "Not a big deal. He's worried about the case too."

"I get that," I say. "He wasn't my biggest fan back in the day, either, if I'm remembering correctly."

Swallowing, Landon smirks. "He was just pissed that you told Miss Haggerty that he was the one who pranked her office with all those fish."

"Well, she was suspecting Pompom, so I had no choice," I shoot back.

Landon shrugs. "Nolan had it coming. He tormented that poor woman. Although, I'm pretty sure she did suspend him for wearing a shirt that looked like a gang slogan but was actually some profound Japanese quote about the afterlife."

We chuckle. My phone goes off.

One look at the message, and I get up.

"Sorry," I tell Landon, "but I have to go."

CHAPTER 17

Kyra

God, I hope she's OK.

Madison doesn't get sick. Ever. But barfing and not being able to stop?

And why was my mom the first to hear about it and not me?

Whatever. I'm pretty sure the vice-principal is so-so on me, since I'm a working single mom and don't return all of her calls within five minutes.

In any case, I'm on my way there now, weaving through cars like I'm getting paid for it. I dare a cop to stop me right now.

It sucks having to leave Landon like that, but I have to get to Mom's place ASAP. Make sure my baby is OK.

This is what being a parent is. Madison will always be my number-one priority. No exceptions.

If Landon can't handle that, well...

Once I get to the door, Mom answers with a gentle smile. "She's asleep."

"What?!? I thought you said she was projectile vomiting and wouldn't stop."

"That was fifteen minutes ago," Mom says, stepping aside so I can come in. "Go see for yourself."

So I do. Sure enough, plopped on Mom's couch, with her hair pulled back from her pale face, Maddy's out like a light.

"What do you think it was?" I ask her.

"Eh, about that," Mom begins, looking distinctly guilty.

"Mom," I say.

She sighs. "Well, I looked it up online, and apparently the hot dogs I gave her last night were recalled yesterday. I'm so sorry."

I give her a small hug and a pat. "It's fine. Could've happened to anyone."

"I am mad, though," Mom says. "Maddy could've been seriously hurt! Shame on them. Good you could come so quickly, dear. Court case done?"

"For the day, yes," I say.

Mom always has had a nose for sniffing out things I don't want her to know about. But I'm not about to admit where I've been. It's messing up my head enough without adding my mom's unwanted input to it.

I end up staying for another few hours, Mom and I catching up, and me helping her with some gardening, until Maddy wakes up. Then, after way too much hugging and "Mommmmm"s, I drive her home, feed her some banana and arrowroot cookies, then tuck her into bed. She's only too happy to sleep some more.

I've just finished the dishes when Pamela calls. "You down for a girl's night?"

"Am I ever!" It seems like ages since we last had one, though I know it hasn't been all that long. I guess a lot just happened. "You OK for here?"

"Of course - see you in five."

Within seconds of me opening the door, Pamela, decked out in her lime green sweats, fixes me with a knowing smile. "You look good. Glowing."

"Thanks, I..." I trail off.

Oh, who am I kidding? I haven't switched up anything in my lazy-person beauty routine. In fact, nothing's changed except that now Landon knows about Madison. And now that I'm actually taking the time to think about it, that's a hell of a relief.

We hug and, after separating, Pompom takes out a DVD and waves it around so much her ponytail braid bounces. "Look what I have..."

"It's that kind of night?" I ask with my own knowing smile.

"I'm in the mood to believe in love again," Pompom says in a low, sultry voice, holding it tight against her chest, eyes closed. She grins. "And let's get real: The Notebook is an every kind of night movie."

"You've got that right," I say, heading for the kitchen. "I'll get the popcorn."

We're a good way through, at the part when they're saying goodbye, when Pompom says, "OK. Spill."

"It's Landon," I confess. "I finally told him about Maddy."

Pompom pauses the movie to turn to me with an excited grin. "And?"

"And he wants to meet her," I say, trying not to smile and failing.

"Ah!" Pompom bounces up and down on the couch before pausing. "Sorry, are we not happy about this?"

"I'm just not sure I'm ready," I admit.

Although part of me feels like bouncing up and down on the couch myself.

"Totally fair," Pompom says, reaching over to give my hand a squeeze. "You're just being a protective Mama Bear."

"And there's this whole case thing that's making things complicated," I admit. "If they found out..."

"Hey." Pompom passes the popcorn bag my way with a stern look. "You're a great lawyer. Even if you lost this case, you'd get another."

"With time, maybe, yeah. But Goldtree Inc. is a big client. It wouldn't look good if it came out that I was dating the opposing team. Definitely not for them, and not for future clients either. In my business, reputation is a big deal."

"True." Pamela shrugs. "I don't know, though, ending it seems so..."

"Obviously the right thing to do?" I finish with a sigh and a sad smile. "I wish I could. For now, I guess I can just hope that things don't work out. Soon."

Pompom snorts. "Please. You're not actually hoping for that."

"I know," I admit. "But I can hope that one day I'll hope for that."

She rolls her eyes. I sigh. "You're right, I'm being an idiot. And - "

My phone rings. Oh... shit.

I'd completely forgotten to tell him what was going on. But it felt nice, this distance. Reassuring. Like I was starting to get my head on straight. Or straighter, anyway.

I sit there and hold the phone like it's a bomb.

"You gonna take that?" Pamela asks with an evil smile.

"Nah," I say. "It's girl's night and - "

"I don't mind."

"Really, it's fine. I don't need to - "

"Just take it," Pompom urges me.

"I can just message him."

Pamela presses the talk button.

"You bitch," I hiss at her.

"Hello?" Landon says. "Kyra?"

I walk off to the kitchen.

"Hey," I say.

"Hey, is everything OK?" Landon asks. "You just raced off..."

"Yeah, I'm really sorry about that. It was Madison. She was throwing up, so I had to get there fast."

"Oh. Right. But she's OK now?"

"Yeah, she's totally fine. Sorry, it was such a crazy day that it slipped my mind to call you."

And I was avoiding you.

"Glad she's alright. Should I come over?"

"No. Pompom's here."

"Tomorrow then?"

"Landon."

"Is it too much to ask to see you every day?" he jokes.

"Yes," I reply. Although my brain is trilling no, of course not! Not at alllll! "I have a kid. A job. Responsibilities."

"Which I have no intention of keeping you from," he says with good humor. "Let me come over tomorrow."

"I'll think about it. Good night, Landon."

"You can't talk for more than a minute?" he growls.

OK. Maybe I have been acting a bit unfair.

"Not much to report," I say. "Just watching The Notebook. Eating popcorn. Catching up with Pamela."

"Alright, I'll let you go." Typical Landon - pushes for what he wants, then makes sure to end things on his own terms. "Goodnight Kyra."

Then again, I should probably just stop overthinking everything. Maybe he's just being agreeable after I tried to hurry off the phone call.

"Night, Landon," I say.

"Well, that went well," Pompom says blithely after I've hung up.

"It did, actually," I say, exhaling. "Kind of."

"So, are you seeing him tomorrow or not?" she asks with an evil smile.

I give her my own sweet smile. "I don't see how that's your business?"

Pompom chucks a decorative pillow at me. "Come off it. You know you'll agree to see him."

"No." I won't smile - I won't. "I don't know if it's a good idea."

Pompom looks to the heavens with an expression of utter exasperation, then gestures to the TV with the remote control. "Fine. Suit yourself. Me, I'd like to watch a non-frustrating love story unfold if that's OK?"

OK, now I'm smiling. "Let's do it."

**

The next day, I let Madison stay home from school. She seems mostly better, but she's still a bit weak and I don't want to take any chances.

We spend the day doing crafts with the help of some rainbow construction paper and kid scissors, as well as a few addition and subtraction exercises from the math workbook she's been avoiding.

For dinner, I cook up some dino buddies and broccoli, and as we're eating-

Ding-dong

"Probably just a Jehovah's Witness," I say, not moving.

"Or Girl Scouts," Madison says, her dino buddy-filled cheeks spread into an excited smile.

"Yes, we'll get the cookies at the grocery store next time, I promise," I tell her.

Ding-dong

"Fine," I say, getting up and heading for the door at her pointed look. "If it's Girl Scouts I'll just buy the cookies now."

"Woohoo!" Madison says.

I open the door and gape at what I find.

"What are you doing here?" I hiss.

Landon smiles apologetically. "Sorry. Just - you weren't responding and I thought..." He frowns. "Sorry."

All I can do is stare at him and wonder what on earth to say. Whoever I was expecting at the door, it definitely wasn't him.

"I can just go," he says.

"Mom?" Madison calls from the kitchen. "Make sure you get the chocolate ones, OK?"

I pause. Landon's uncertain eyes meet mine.

"OK, fine," I grumble, opening the door wide to let him in. "But just for an hour."

"Just for an hour," Landon answers with something of a smile.

Once I close the door behind him, I can feel my heart beating through my chest. This is it. The moment I've been dreading. Looking forward to. The one I'm not at all ready for.

He smells good - too good.

Ugh. I want to hug him and sink into those arms, escape. But I can't.

I have to keep my wits about me. If this doesn't work...

I walk into the kitchen, Landon following behind.

"Maddy," I say, trying to keep my voice as casual as possible, "there's someone I want you to meet."

And then we're standing there, me in my fuzzy flip-flops, Landon with his shoes still on, looking how I've never seen him look: sheepish and shy and uncertain and eager all at once.

"This is Landon," I say. "My friend."

Madison, midway through having one dino buddy attack another, glances up. "Oh. Hi." Her lips press together as her hazel-eyed gaze goes to Landon. "You're not supposed to wear shoes inside the house, you know." Then she holds her pink sparkly-nailed finger to her lips. "I won't tell Mom, though."

Landon laughs. "Thanks for keeping it on the DL."

"We're having dino buddies with broccoli," I tell Landon, "Want some?"

"Sure." He grins. "Got to take off my shoes first, though."

When he comes back, Madison fixes him with a curious look. "You don't actually like broccoli, do you?"

"Yeah, I do," Landon replies. "Why not?"

"Because it's... well... ick." Madison makes a face.

Landon chuckles. "It's not that bad."

Madison extends her broccoli-stabbed fork his way. "Want mine, then?"

"Madison," I scold her.

She exhales, bringing her fork back to her plate. "Sorry, Mom. But it really is gross. Plus, Janie told me her parents don't make her eat any vegetables at all."

"Yes, and we aren't Janie's family in this house, now are we?"

"Nooo, Mom."

Landon and I exchange an amused look. "Kids these days."

"Didn't know you were a grand chef," Landon teases.

"What can I say," I joke, "gourmet dino buddies from the package are my specialty."

Chewing and swallowing his, Landon nods. "I can see that."

Once we're almost finished eating, Madison puts her dishes in the sink before looking my way. "Are we still marble painting tonight?"

"I..." I pause. No reason to put it off just because Landon's here.

Landon nudges me. "Sounds like fun. Mind if I crash your paint party?"

"Sure," Madison says. "Just make sure not to use the big teal marble, OK?"

"Sure. That your favorite?"

"Yeah. It was my dad's," she says easily.

Oh shit.

"Oh." Landon blinks. "Right. Fair enough. I used to have marbles myself, so I get it."

As we set up the canvases, paint and marbles on the back lawn outside while Maddy plays with her Beanie Babies inside, Landon smiles at me. "Madison's pretty awesome."

"Thanks," I say, trying to keep the relief out of my voice.

Although it has been less than an hour that he's been here. I shouldn't jump to conclusions about this working or not. Plus, it's less about Landon getting along with Madison than about Madison getting along with Landon.

"About her dad..." he begins hesitantly.

"I don't want to talk about it," I snap. I sink onto the wooden step of the back porch, letting a long slow exhale roll out of my throat. It's a bit cold out here. I should be getting a sweatshirt.

As I'm heading in to get one, I realize that I've left Landon standing there, looking more than a bit sheepish.

"One thing at a time, OK?" I say.

"Just... don't want to say the wrong thing," he says.

Aw, he looks so glum. I almost feel bad. I rise and squeeze his hand. "Hey. It's OK. You're doing fine."

"Good." He swallows, musters up a smile. "I'm way out of my depth here. But good."

Just then Madison bursts out, running at top speed and then skidding to a stop in front of our set-up. "Whoa. Cool."

"You ready to get started?" I ask her.

Plopped on her butt already, taking out a marble, she grins. "I'm ready!"

An hour or so later, our hands are paint-splattered, our canvases paint-covered and we're out of purple paint, but we've done it. We've done the marble paint craft, and it's Madison's bedtime.

"Time for bed," I tell her.

She groans. "Mom. Can't I hang out with you and your friend a bit longer? He's cool."

Behind her, Landon points to her, grinning and nodding emphatically, and mouths: I'm cool.

I roll my eyes. "Nope. You were sick just the other day. You need all the sleep you can get."

"Ugh," Madison groans again, although she's heading inside. At the door, she pauses, "Was Landon your boyfriend?"

I pause. "Why do you ask that?"

"He was just in a bunch of Mom's pictures in her photo album," Madison says before disappearing inside.

I stand there a few seconds. I can't tell what I'm feeling. Can't even tell what I'm thinking.

"Yes, he was," I say, following her inside. "But that was a long time ago."

"OK, Mom," she says, then leaves to brush her teeth.

The rest of the night is more surrealness: Landon helps out reading Madison a story - Babar Gets Groceries.

I can't stop giggling at Landon's put-on falsetto voice for Queen Celeste.

Then, all at once, it's just the two of us standing in the hallway outside.

"That was fun," Landon says. "Guess I'll be seeing you?"

"You've got somewhere to be?" I ask, careful not to let the sinking of my gut sound in my voice.

"No." He pauses, can't seem to let himself look at me. "Just - seeing you today was enough for me. Don't want you thinking I'm here for something more."

Aw!

Maybe it really is the same for him as it is for me. How, when I catch his eye, let myself look at him for too long, I can't think. Can hardly breathe.

"You sure?" I ask.

"Not really," he says with a small smile as he heads for the door.

There, after he's put on his shoes, he says, "See you, Kyra."

"See you, Landon," I say.

And then he leaves.

I stand there, in the doorway, listening to his car start up and drive away.

Not even a goodbye kiss...

And yet the butterflies in my chest are doing the can-can as if we did that and more. In a way, we did.

Today worked. We worked. Me, and Landon, and Maddy...

I head for the kitchen wearing what's probably a stupid smile, although I'm not about to hang around mooning over it.

Better not to think about it. Not yet, anyway.

First, I get some long-overdue house errands and cleaning done. I'm just about to get started brushing my own teeth when my phone rings.

It's Landon.

"I just wanted to tell you that I get it now," he says. "Why you wanted to protect your daughter. She's pretty special."

"Thanks," I say, "but - "

"I'm not finished yet. I want you to know that I'd like to be a part of both of your lives - if you'll let me."

...Is he actually saying this?

...He's actually saying this.

...And what am I going to say about it?

"Kyra?" he says.

"OK," I say.

It's all I can say. I can't even begin to process this, what I think about it, what I should think about it. It seems like every time my mind starts to at all catch up, events outpace it even more.

"I know it's a big thing to say now, and it's still way early," he says. "I don't expect an answer now or even soon. I just wanted you to know where I see myself standing now."

"OK."

There I go again...

"Although I do have one request," he adds.

My heart drops. Here it is. Classic Landon.

Give a little and take a whole lot more.

CHAPTER 18

Landon

"I haven't even agreed that we're getting back together," Kyra points out smoothly.

"Hear me out," I say. "Rex Tygone, the director of Disney World, is an old friend of Dad's. He sends us about ten free Disney World passes every year. I'd like to take you and Madison this weekend."

Silence.

I glare at the half-finished stir-fry on the table in front of me.

Shit.

Emerson just reminded me about the passes this afternoon. But it was an idiot move, telling her right now. I could've waited on it.

"You don't have to do that," Kyra says, voice still guarded.

"I want to."

Take it back while you still can.

"I don't know," she says.

Too late - just run with it.

"You don't have to. There's a few more days in the week. Anyway, my brothers are going, Harley too. Thought it could be fun."

"If Goldtree Inc. found out - "

"How would they find out?" I ask her. "I'm not about to tell them. Are you?"

"No, but it's not that simple, Landon."

"Which is why you have several days to decide."

Now I'm starting to sound like a lawyer myself.

"True," Kyra says.

I pace along my kitchen floor. Fuck.

This conversation is not going how I wanted. Or expected. Not that I expected her to agree immediately.

"If it's such a big deal to you," I point out, "you could pay for you and Madison. I'd rather treat you, but if you insist - "

"I'm going to need to sleep on it, at least," she says.

A pause.

"It is really nice of you to offer, though. Madison's been wanting to go for ages, but we just never found the time."

"Now's the time."

"We'll see," she says, a smile in her voice. "But I do have to go now. Night, Landon."

"Night, Kyra," I say, "Sweet dreams."

And then she's hung up, and it's me and my half-finished stir-fry.

Today was... Weird. Fun.

I've never been a kid guy, but Madison was cool. A tough cookie, just like her mother. There's something familiar about her - but maybe it's just because she has Kyra's dark hair and pale skin.

And this weekend... we'll see.

I end up shooting a text to Greyson: Kyra and her daughter may come this weekend.

Who knows, maybe he or Harley knows some good activities for kids. God knows I'm clueless.

I end up passing out on the couch and awaking to a knock.

What the hell time is it?

I peer through the peephole, and, seeing who it is, groan.

"This is a brothertervention," Nolan says, striding in as soon as I open the door.

He's wearing matching red sweats with white lines down the sides, his long hair pulled into a man bun, and a firm grin that I know is going to give me grief.

"Hello to you too," I say, annoyed already.

"Sorry," Emerson says, the expression on his blond head a bit sheepish. He's dressed in his usual khakis and pastel button-up. "Nolan said it was an emergency."

Nolan spins around to glare at me. "You are not taking her on our annual Storm Disney Trip."

My glare goes to Greyson, who looks as weary as I'm feeling. "You told them."

He shrugs. "I didn't know it was some big secret. They would've found out when she showed up, anyway."

"Why are you even still dating her, bro?" Nolan demands, sitting in my seat and starting on my stir-fry. "That woman is bad news. And she has a kid."

"I've got the situation handled," I say tersely.

"Then why are we losing the court case?" Nolan shoots back. "Handled means winning. This woman is doing cartwheels around us in there."

"Could it maybe have something to do with the fact that Dad is guilty?" My voice is rising though I didn't intend it to. "That maybe now some of his past transgressions are finally catching up with us?"

"Fuck off." Nolan fixes me with an angry glare. "Are you a Storm or not?"

"I am," I say, glaring right back at him. Sometimes it's disconcerting, seeing him with the same expression I have. Like looking into a mirror. "Which doesn't mean I have to deny facts. I'm not prepared to make the same mistakes as Dad - are you?"

Nolan looks away, muttering, "You're missing the point."

"Landon does have a point," Greyson says levelly. "This might be on Dad. Making poor choices."

"Are you kidding me?" Nolan asks, turning to him so fast that his man bun bobs a bit. "You could lose your show over this."

"I don't want the show if it's based on a lie," Greyson says firmly.

Nolan exhales long and low as he looks from Greyson to me. "Jesus. Women. They screw with your head."

"Maybe we should go?" Emerson suggests tentatively.

"Giving up already?" Nolan says derisively. His glare travels around the room. "C'mon guys. We're supposed to be brothers. A team. Are we really giving up on Dad that easy?"

"We're not giving up on him," I state. "We're just facing the facts. I loved Dad as much of any of you, but he was human. He did some not-great things. He was a maverick and a media giant, but he still did some fucked-up, stupid things too. Like the whole tax debacle. C'mon Nolan, these plagiarism charges aren't that much of a stretch and you know it."

He won't meet my eye. "All I know is that Storm Inc. can't afford much more bad publicity. This is our inheritance and Dad's legacy on the line."

"I won't let us go down," I say simply.

"It might not be up to you," Nolan shoots back. "This is a downward spiral, and if we don't stop it somewhere along the line, we're going to find all of ourselves drowned. Dad deserves better than that. We do."

"What would you have me do, then?" I say, sitting down and grabbing back my stir-fry. All this arguing is making me damn hungry. "I have the best lawyer we've got on the case."

"I don't know, how about stop sleeping with the enemy, for starters," Nolan says, yanking the stir-fry back in front of him. "And assuming Dad is innocent until he's proven guilty?"

"I'm not assuming he's guilty," I say quietly. "And I won't stop seeing her."

Nolan shakes his head, gaping at me like I've just told him three plus three is seven. "You're a lost cause, you know that? This woman already almost ruined your life once, now you're going to let her do it again." He rises. "Be my guest. But don't think I'm about to sit and watch."

He makes for the door.

"So I won't be seeing you at Disney World, I guess?" I say.

He glances back at me and shakes his head, but all Nolan says as he leaves is, "Don't say I didn't warn you."

"Sorry," Emerson says, ducking my gaze. "But I should get going too. Early start - there's this new Debussy piece that's kicking my ass and..." He pauses. "Just - I don't agree with what he said. Not completely. Only... be careful, will you?"

"Of course," I say, but he's already turning away.

"Apologies for barging in like this. Have a good night."

And then it's just me and Greyson, looking at each other.

"He's just trying to look out for you, you know," he says. "He doesn't understand it."

"He's never been in love, I know," I grumble. "Which doesn't make him trying to control my life OK."

"You know Nolan, he's always been a bit of a drama queen," Greyson says with a little chuckle. "Don't let it get to you. But don't dismiss it out of hand, either - it would be a damn shame for us to lose the show and be embroiled in another media scandal if we could avoid it."

"I'm not taking this lightly," I state. "I've as much to lose as any of you."

"I know." Greyson's searching my face, frowning slightly. "And I know you can't change who you fall for."

"Don't know if I'd go that far."

"C'mon, Landon. You're telling me you're pushing this thing with Kyra just because she's a good lay?"

I grab the stir-fry, start eating.

"Suit yourself," Greyson says, rising. "Will we be seeing you this weekend?"

"Maybe," I say.

"Alright." He comes over to pat me on the shoulder. "You take care of yourself, OK?"

"You too."

And then he's gone, and it's just me and my stir-fry. And the thoughts I've been avoiding.

About the weekend. About her.

CHAPTER 19

Kyra

"Your friend was nice," Madison says as she puts on her pink and blue duck socks. "Will he come over another time?"

"We'll see," I say. "Now, chop chop. Less talking, more sock-putting-on. We're running short on time."

"OK." She frowns. "Being late isn't the end of the world, you know."

"Madison." I pull back to look her right in the face. Normally, she's the one bothering me to hurry up and get her to school. She loves school. "Is something wrong?"

But all I see is a blank face and a smudge of crumbs - there, got it - that needed wiping. "Nope."

"OK... but you'd tell me if there were?"

Madison heads for the door. "Mom. We're going to be late."

"OK," I say, uneasy.

But Madison's like a turtle if she doesn't want to tell you something. And we are short on time, so the best thing is probably to leave it for now.

That afternoon, I get a call from the school principal, Mrs. O'Melly.

"Ms. Masterson, we have some unfortunate news. Madison has locked herself in the bathroom and won't come out."

"What?" I say.

"You should come here immediately."

Once I get there, I find that they've already managed to coax Madison out, albeit with the promise of some Doritos I end up supplying. As we sit in the principal's astringent-smelling, obsessively orderly brown-tone office, I hear the full story, partly from Mrs. O'Melly, partly from Madison herself. After weeks of being bullied by another girl, Amelia, my daughter had had enough and decided to barricade herself in the bathroom. This was the first the school was hearing about it too, apparently.

"We will be disciplining Amelia," Mrs. O'Melly says once Madison has told her side of the story. The principal's prolific salt and pepper eyebrows are lowered in an expression of utter ferocity. I definitely wouldn't want to be on the receiving end of that look. Fortunately, her eyebrows soften as she looks my way. "But it may be best to have Madison take the rest of the week off. A bit of a break might do her some good. Maybe even a little trip? Kids often don't need much to bounce back from these things."

"Sounds like a good idea," I tell her, shaking her hand on the way out.

On the car ride home, Madison is quiet.

"Hey, what do you think about your principal's suggestion?" I ask.

"Sure," Maddy says, her voice flat.

"Madison."

"It could be fun," she admits with a small smile my way before turning back to the car window.

I try turning on the radio, but somehow Nelly Furtado's 'I'm Like a Bird' only makes the quiet loom even bigger.

"Why didn't you tell me?" I finally ask her.

No use in putting it off any more.

"I didn't want you to worry," she says.

"I'm sorry," she adds.

"Maddy." I pull over the car so she can have my full attention. "I'm your mom. It's my job to worry. And help out when I can. But I can't help you if I don't know something's wrong."

No response.

I reach over to give her hand a tentative squeeze. "OK, honey?"

"OK, Mom," she says dutifully.

Clearly, she's not in the mood. Not that I blame her. When I first got there, her eyes were dry but red from recent crying. Her favorite locket was broken, courtesy of that little red-haired demon Amelia. Needless to say, it has not been a good day, and there's no point in pretending that I can make it all better with a kind word or a hug.

I know Maddy. When she's sad, her favorite thing in the world is to go to bed, get under the covers, and fall asleep. The sooner I get us home, the better.

Pulling back onto the street, I stare at the windshield dully.

Weeks. This has been going on for weeks. How could I have missed it? Is Madison really that good of an actor, or was I too wrapped up with the whole Landon situation? Am I a shitty mother who's only concerned about herself?

And, is it crazy that as soon as Mrs. O'Melly said 'trip' I thought: like Disney World?

After a nice long nap, Maddy and I spend the rest of the day going over some English lessons in her workbook. If we go, she's likely to miss them, and a few extra. And getting a bit ahead never hurt anyway.

While I'm tucking her in that night, Maddy takes my hand. "Don't worry, Mom. I'll be fine."

A sad little laugh comes out of me. "I just wish you could've told me."

"I know."

"Maddy..."

"Yeah?"

"What would you say if we went to Disney World this weekend?"

Maddy's eyes snap open and she sits up straight in her bed. "You're joking."

"It's just a thought," I say, a bit taken aback.

While I had expected some excitement, I hadn't expected this much.

She grabs my hand with both of hers. "Could we? Please?"

I haven't seen her this excited since last Christmas, when Santa got her a Barbie Dream House.

"OK," I find myself saying. "Fine. Let's do it."

"Really?"

"Really."

"Mom!" She leaps onto her bed and starts bouncing. "We're going to Disney World! We're going to Disney World! We're going to Disney! Disney! Disney!"

"You crazy little monkey," I say, laughing and hugging her.

Next thing I know, I'm right up there jumping on the creaking bed beside her. Thank God I splurged mandd got the sturdier $200-morre frame.

Maybe this is just what she needs - what I need. Heck, when was the last time I took a weekend trip?

Maybe this could be a really good thing for both of us.

Even if the whole Landon element is freaking me the hell out.

As soon as I've gotten Madison calmed down enough to tuck her in and am out of the room, I call up Landon.

Better make sure this plan is 100% on before getting Maddy's hopes up any more. Although, if it's not, I might just take her there myself.

"Hey," I say, "how's it going?"

"Great," he says. "What about you? You sound exhausted."

"Guess I am," I say, realizing it as I say it. "I had to go get Maddy from school early today."

"Oh. Something wrong?"

"She locked herself in the bathroom to escape her bully."

"Shit. She OK?"

"She's fine," I say. "The principal is going to discipline the girl responsible, but she suggested that Maddy take a few days off school. Maybe even go on a little trip."

I can hear the smile in Landon's voice as he says, "Like a trip to Disney World?"

"I may have mentioned it to her."

"So, you'll go?" he asks.

"Yes," I say, "but I'm footing the bill. I don't want anything on record that could be misconstrued as you paying me off."

"You're winning the case and probably will win the case," Landon points out. "And if I'd be paying you off for anything, it would be for spending time with me."

He pauses. "OK, that came out wrong."

I just laugh. "When are you guys flying in? Maddy and I can try to get a plane around the same time. And are you staying in the actual park?"

The next few minutes we spend back-and-forthing different hotel suggestions and flight options. Finally, we settle on flying in Friday night, and staying at the Four Seasons right in Disney World.

"Guess that's it," Landon says.

"Guess so," I say.

I try and fail to think of something else to say to keep the conversation going.

"Pamela coming over tonight?" Landon asks.

"No."

"Any other plans?"

"Maybe start packing for the trip. Usually I leave it to the last minute."

"Want company?"

I let out a little uncertain laugh. "For packing?"

"For anything, really."

God, what that voice of his does to me, the excitement just a suggestion of his can bring me...

He exhales. "Can I see you tonight?"

I pause.

Do I want to see him? Yes. Should I see him? Why not?

Things are going so well, and when he gets close, I...

"I miss you," he says.

"Let me come over," he says.

My wall of self-control crumbles.

"I miss you too," I admit, "And fine, but just for an hour or so. And no sleepovers."

"Wouldn't dream of it," Landon says in a voice that I can tell is coming out of a wolfish smile. "See you in 15."

'15' is just enough time to change out of my ugly slacks into my cute ones and give my teeth a quick brush (the fish sticks we had for dinner tonight wouldn't do me any favors). Before I know it, my phone is ringing.

It's Landon, at the door. "Wasn't sure I should ring the bell," he explains. "Since Madison's asleep."

"Oh, that girl?" I say with a little laugh. "She'd sleep through the apocalypse."

"In that case," he says.

Ding-dong

"Don't freak out," he says when I open the door. "But I come bearing gifts."

My jaw manages to drop and grin at the same time at what I see: two bouquets of red roses. One big, one small.

"You trying to bribe my child into liking you?" I joke.

"She already likes me," Landon shoots back.

"Thank you, though!" I say, wrapping my arms around him.

"I'm just glad I get to see you," he says, wrapping his arms around me.

As soon as they close around my back, all the tension of the day falls away. Everything does.

God, being in his arms feels so good, safe. He feels so good. And that warm piney musk of his, settling over me like a balm...

Hell, I adore this man.

Whoa there, Ky...

But it's true. Every time we touch, everything softens. Straightens out. Clears up. I should be with him. Need to be.

Hang the hell on there...

I pull away with a smile that hopefully doesn't give away my crazy-person thoughts. "You probably want to come inside."

A gentle smile. "That would be nice."

As I let him in, it occurs to me that we never talked about what we'd do once he got here. And that that, in itself, could suggest something.

"I'll put these in water," I say, bustling away with the two bouquets.

Madison's first bouquet. She's going to love it.

Really, I'm buying myself some time. If Landon tries for... that... I'm not sure I can say no. I've missed him. My body has missed him.

But things are going so well. I don't want to jinx things.

"There's a new Bond movie out," he says. "If you're interested?"

"Sounds good to me," I say, heading to the TV room gratefully.

That's another thing I've always loved about Landon. He always takes charge. Knows what to do.

The latest Bond movie is as exciting and funny as I'd hope. The couch we're on is comfortable, but what's even more comfortable is cuddling with Landon, resting with my head on his chest.

"You know," he says, eyeing me thoughtfully as the credits role. "You could be a Bond girl."

"You mean I could kick your ass?" I joke.

"That too," he says. "But mostly that you're classy, pretty, a damn terrific partner."

"What if I don't want to be the partner?" I joke, "What if I want to be the leading lady?"

"Then Superwoman or Catwoman might be more for you," he jokes back. "And in that case, I'll be Superman or Batman."

God, that smile of his is addictive. Has he always had the slightest of dimples?

"Oh yeah?" I say.

"Oh yeah," he says.

Our lips entwine and say the rest. His hands cup my face as his lips and tongue sweep with mine - I've missed you, I've needed this, I've been waiting all night for this.

He pulls away, an odd twist to his lips. "Only you, I swear."

"Only me what?"

He gestures to what I'm wearing. "Could make sweat pants as tempting as lingerie."

"Sorry?" I ask with a devilish smirk.

Our lips meet again. His hands thread through my hair and pull, ever so slightly. Mine do the same. He tastes like the extra butter Orville Redenbacher popcorn we made, and the banana-strawberry smoothie we shared afterwards. He's touching me, stroking me gingerly, as though afraid of what would happen if he dared caress me how he wanted to.

He pulls away, gets up.

"I want to stay, Kyra... but you said no sleepovers?" His questioning look is strained; clearly, it's taking all the self-control he has not to pounce back on me and pick up where we left off.

"Yes, it's probably..." I take a breath. Concentrate, Ky. "Probably for the best."

He nods. Looks away. "I should go."

He makes for the door.

"That's it?" I ask after him. "You're just going to storm out of here?"

There it is again, him going cold with me for seemingly no reason.

He rounds on me with a scowl. "What do you want from me, Kyra? To respect your wishes or to do what I want? Because I can't do both. I'm trying to do the right thing here."

I know I'm being unfair, unreasonable. But I can't stop myself. I want him to stay. I want him to leave. "By leaving without so much as a goodbye?"

"No." Still he won't look at me. "By leaving before I take you how I want to."

His words spark in the air.

"OK," I say.

"OK," he says.

"So, no goodbye kiss then?" I can't resist asking.

He pauses. "Damn. You're really not going to make this easy for me, are you?"

CHAPTER 20

Landon

"That a no?" she teases.

Fuck - that's a yes.

Yes, I'll have that kiss - and you. I'll kiss your clothes off, kiss you moaning. Kiss you mine.

"That's a no," I say. "Goodnight, Kyra."

And then I leave. Because anything else would end up with me in her bed. Of course, that's what I want. But that's not the only thing I want.

I want to do the right thing this time.

**

Back at home, I can't get her out of my head. I can hardly sleep, hardly eat. Even the next day, trying to get some work done at the office does little good. I have to turn off my phone so I won't call her. Block the internet so I won't look up random useless webpages of her.

Too bad I can't block her from my brain - her hurt face at the end last night, how good she felt in my arms before that.

When Greyson suggests we go for lunch, I jump at the opportunity.

"You seem... distracted," he says after we've arrived at Beckta, ordered and eaten and drunk a bit in its airy window-filled room. "Happy but distracted."

"Lot going on," I say simply.

"It's OK if it's her," he says. "She give you an answer for Disney World?"

"She's coming," I say.

"Nolan won't be happy," Greyson says, a wry twist to his mouth and amusement in his blue eyes. He has a new light beard that matches his tousled hair - Harley's request, apparently. "Then again, he already planned to sit this one out as, and I quote, 'an act of protest'."

I roll my eyes. "Emerson?"

"Doesn't want to get in the middle of this," Greyson returns. "Plus, he figures - and rightly - that he'd be the fifth wheel. The only one without a date. The girl he's seeing is just casual, so he doesn't want to go there with her."

"Guess that's fair."

"What about work?" Greyson asks. "How's the whole President thing going?"

"About the same," I admit. "Feeling less like I'm out of my depth every day."

Greyson chuckles. "That's the spirit. Remember, if you need any advice, I'm here."

"I may have one question." I frown. I didn't plan on saying anything, but it just slipped out, so might as well. "When the whole thing with Harley was going down, how did you..."

"Focus on work?" Greyson laughs. "Easy: I didn't. Probably wasn't the greatest President for those first few heated weeks between us, but what can you do? That's love for you."

I avoid his knowing gaze.

"You want my advice on the whole Kyra dilemma?" he asks.

"Not really," I say.

"Too bad," he says. "You really like her? Don't mess this up."

"That isn't advice," I scoff, sipping my Screwdriver.

I low-key mocked Greyson when he ordered us drinks at noon, but this is coming in handy. God knows I need something to take the edge off.

"Don't be afraid to try to make it work with her," he's saying now. "And be honest with her."

"What does it look like I'm doing?"

"I just know that last time - "

"We're not talking about last time."

"Did you even tell her about it?"

I down the whole drink, glaring at him over the rim. "What difference does that make?"

Greyson sips his own drink. "You tell me."

I don't like where this conversation is taking us.

"About Disney World," I say. "You got any preferences?"

"I know Harley was wanting to check out Epcot, but not really, no," Greyson says. "You?"

"I'm game for whatever Kyra and Madison want to do."

"Madison," Greyson says thoughtfully. "So, that's her daughter?"

"Yep."

"What's she like?"

"She's cool. Funny. Cute."

"The father?"

"Not in the picture. Kyra won't tell me anything about him."

"Maybe he was a rebound," Greyson suggests. "Since the kid is what, nine?"

"Yeah."

I bite at the remainder of cantaloupe I left. "How are things with you and Harley?"

"Being a dad is tricky," Greyson says. "But Harley's great. No complaints here."

He stretches, smiling like a damn fool.

Although it suits him - married life. He almost makes it look appealing, settling down, having a kid. Almost.

"Yeah, yeah, you're the poster boy for marital bliss," I tell him, "but I should get going. I have some ladies to visit. I can pay on my way out."

"Fair enough," Greyson says, rising. "But I can get the bill this time. Just - Landon?"

"Yeah?"

"Be careful."

I give him a quick back-patting hug. "Thanks, old man. See you at the airport."

"See you - don't be late."

"That was one time - and that was Nolan's fault."

"Yeah, yeah."

**

It turns out that Kyra and Madison are out, so I end up going back to my place to pack.

The next few days pass in a quick blur. Before I know it, I'm in a cab pulled up to their place, with a duffel bag of my stuff at my feet.

"Hello, stranger," Kyra says, after she's loaded her and Maddy's luggage into the trunk.

She's wearing a loose teal shirt that's slightly sheer - sheer enough to get me excited.

Although I put that thought away - for now.

"Hey there," Maddy says.

"You're looking Florida ready," I say, pointing to her hat with Minnie Mouse ears.

She giggles. "Where's yours?"

I pat my duffel bag. "Mine's a special hat, though."

"Oh yeah?"

"Yeah - it's indestructible."

"No way." Her eyes slit with delighted suspicion.

"Yeah way," I tell her, "Even if an elephant eats it, it comes out whole."

"Liar!" she declares with a delighted giggle.

"Madison," Kyra scolds, although she's frowning at me. "What's up with you?"

"It's true," I say, unzipping my pack and handing the army green hat, top side down, to Madison. Then I show her the webpage describing the story of how it has been eaten by an elephant and come out fully intact - three different times. "Take a look."

A minute or so of intent reading, and she lets out a delighted peal of laughter. "I can't believe it. That's insane."

"That's the Tilley hat for you. It's an adventurer's hat."

Maddy brightens even more. "Does that mean we're going to go on adventures?"

"Oh, definitely. Didn't your mom tell you? There's three parks we're going to go to, and they're huge. They've got rides, animals, restaurants."

"We can go to restaurants at home," Maddy says, clearly unimpressed.

"Can you see elephants at home?" I shoot back.

All smiles again. "The same elephants that ate the hat?"

"Not sure. Want to ask them with me?"

Madison and Kyra just laugh and laugh. I'm smiling myself. I never had a ride to the airport as much fun as this.

Before I know it, we're there. I managed to ensure that Kyra and Maddy were on the same flight as me, so we go through security together.

Once we're out, I buy us all some fried plantains and we sit down to wait. Madison has a book - some Harry Potter. Kyra has her own book - something by Kate Morton.

"It any good?" I ask her.

"It is," she admits, "but I can't really concentrate. I'm too excited."

"Dying to see the elephants too?" I tease.

"No, just excited to see how much fun Maddy's going to have." Hell, she's beaming. Damn do I love making my girl happy - not that she is my girl. Not yet, at least. "And a spa day won't hurt."

I smile. "Ah, so you did check out that email I sent last night."

"Sorry." Apologetic smile. "I got it in the middle of a packing frenzy. Madison was convinced she needed to bring just about every pair of shorts she has. Which yes, is over fourteen."

"You were the one who couldn't decide which bathing suit to bring," Madison replies smoothly. "You were all, 'do you think Landon will like this one or this one'?"

"I was not!" Kyra says hotly.

Maddy and I crack up, then high-five each other.

"Oh, so that's how it is?" Kyra says, although she's chuckling now too. "You two against me?"

"No comment," Maddy says with a grin.

The plane is right on time, so we board without any issues. On it, Kyra falls fast asleep. That leaves me and Maddy, half watching Madagascar, and half eating every can of Pringles we can get our hands on. On what must be the fourth, Maddy casts me an assessing sidelong gaze.

"What?" I ask.

"Nothing," she says, all innocence.

"Tell me," I say.

"Make me," she shoots back, sticking out her tongue.

I shrug. "Alright. Guess we're full of Pringles now, is that it?"

Maddy sighs. "Fine. Don't tell Mom I'm telling you this. But I think she really likes you."

"What makes you say that?"

She shrugs. "Dunno. Anyway, you have to promise to keep it a secret."

I do a motion of zipping up my lips and throwing away the key. "You have my word."

The flight is pretty uneventful. Eventually Maddy nods off too. That leaves just me, munching on the remainder of the Pringles.

When we arrive, it's a quick walk through the airport to catch a taxi. It takes us straight to our hotel - the Four Seasons in Disney World. On the outside, it's just a tan, vaguely Spanish block of a building, but on the inside, it's all chic furniture and staff who know what you want before you even know it yourself.

We end up meeting up with Harley and Greyson at the rooftop steakhouse, all dark grey stone and some sort of giant red paper ornament overhead.

"Kyra," Harley says, grinning like she means it as she shakes her hand, "great to finally meet you. I've heard a lot."

"Hopefully mostly good things," Kyra says, only half-joking.

"This guy was always a fan," Harley says with a wink as she leans in. "He thought you were the best thing to happen to our Landon."

"Did I say that?" Greyson grumbles.

"You did," Harley singsongs.

"Remind me not to tell you things," he says, deadpan.

"What about you?" Kyra asks. "How's your little boy - I think Landon told me his name is Dakota?"

"He's having a nice weekend with Grandma," Harley says. "I swear, sometimes I think he loves her more than me. Probably since he gets unlimited cookies at her house."

After some more pleasantries, we sit down, order and start eating.

It feels so easy, natural, being here with them. Harley and Madison hit it off right away.

"I hope I get a little girl just like you," Harley confides in Madison, after cracking up at how Madison moved her fries into the shape of an anteater.

"If you're lucky," Madison says with a giggle.

"If you two ever want babysitting on this trip, just let me know," Harley says.

"Will do," Kyra tells her.

She's wearing the kind of smile that I know from experience is real. I let out a breath I hadn't even realized I was holding in.

This is actually going well.

Before I know it, it's time to take a protesting Madison up for bed. "Mom, we barely saw anything!"

"It's 10:00 PM, Maddy," Kyra says sternly. "Two hours past your bedtime."

"We're on vacation."

"You're exhausted," Kyra says. "I saw you nodding off in the cab ride on the way here."

"Was not."

"I'm not having this argument with you now." She takes Madison's hand. "I promise we can have a grand tour tomorrow - and go on any rides you like."

A sly grin. "Any rides?"

"Any ones you're old enough for."

I rise to join them.

"It's fine," Kyra says, "you enjoy yourself. I'll be back in fifteen."

"I'd rather join," I say, coming along.

Sure enough, up in their room, we've barely read the first page of her Arthur book before Madison's out like a light. Kyra strokes her head with a little chuckle. "I knew that trip tired her right out."

"Her and you both," I say with a smile. "You were conked the whole plane ride."

I take her hand and lead her to a side door. "I need to show you the best part." I open it to show her an even nicer room, all marble floor and black and blue furniture. "Got a room right beside."

"Oh yeah?" she says, making for the bed. She eyes me sleepily. "Think I might... take a nap, if that's OK?"

Although her on that bed has my thoughts going elsewhere, if my girl wants a nap...

Enough with that 'my girl' BS.

"Sure," I tell her.

Now that I'm thinking about it, I'm about to pass out myself. So, I cuddle up next to Kyra's already asleep form and wrap my arms around her, and less than a minute later, I'm asleep myself.

**

When I wake up and look at my phone, I groan. Midnight. So much for sleeping through the night.

"What is it?" Kyra asks with a yawn.

I roll over to eye her. "You awake too?"

She flutters her lashes with a mischievous smirk. "Nope. I'm sleep-talking."

That gets both of us laughing.

"Know what it's the perfect time for?" Kyra asks.

My lips go to hers and she pulls away with a giggle. "OK, point taken. But I was thinking of something else."

I scowl, and she plants a kiss right at the corner of my lips. "Let's check out the pool."

"Right now?"

She quirks an eyebrow. "You got plans?"

"Actually..."

She slaps my oncoming hand away. "Come on. Let's check it out."

"But what about - "

"Harley said she can watch Madison. If she's up, let's do it."

At my hesitation, she continues, "Trust me. After Madison's made us go on every ride in the park, we'll be too exhausted to do anything other than pass out tomorrow night."

I yawn. Part of me's too exhausted to do much now - but then again, the prospect of seeing Kyra in a sexy little swimsuit...

"Here," Kyra says, getting out of bed, "I'll leave so you won't be distracted."

I frown at her. "And if I enjoyed the distraction?"

She's already headed to the closet to change. "Then you'll get more of it when we get to the pool. Maybe."

That's enough to get me shooting Harley a text. She responds almost immediately, is as happy as a husky in snow about the prospect of watching Madison for a bit.

A few minutes of changing, a few more minutes of Kyra going over what to watch out for with Harley - she really is thorough - and we're out of the room walking down the slightly lemon-scented hallway.

"If the pool is as deserted as these hallways..." Kyra trails off as we walk along.

I sneakily cop a feel.

"Landon!" she scolds me.

"Couldn't help it," I grumble. "Maybe if your cover-up actually did its job..."

Kyra tries to glare at me, but just ends up giggling. "Oh, so now this is my fault, is it?"

"Actually, it's your ass's fault, but sure."

She gives me a playful slap, and then we're there.

I press my key card onto the door, then hold it open for her. She saunters in, immediately shrugging off her cover-up.

One glimpse of her curves in that black ribbed bikini and my cock is stiffening.

She casts a coy look back, as though she knows exactly what I'm thinking, though she's pretending not to. "Come on."

I come on. Take her hand, follow her past the massive pool, then further into the back room, separated from the pool by a door. It's a secluded cove with walls of blue, teal and white mosaic and filled with hot bubbling waters.

Seconds after we're both in the steamy water, the last of my self-control rolls away, along with all the tension in my body.

"Come here," I growl.

No more waiting. I'm hard as a fucking brick right now.

Her smile is teasing, though. "Or?"

I'm already wading over there. No more waiting. "I'll come and get you myself."

Next second, our lips are connecting.

Fuck yeah. She tastes good, feels good. Her breasts are full and firm, and her ass...

"I've been waiting to do this all day," I find myself saying.

God, she's hot.

Our hands entwine, and mine drag across her body, under her bathing suit. I cup one breast, then the other, massaging and enjoying them. A perfect handful each.

Her hands drift under the water to my package. A pleased grunt rolls out of my throat.

Fucking yes.

With the flat of my palm, I press her against the tiled wall of the cove, then push aside her bathing suit bottom and shove myself into her.

Yes.

Fuck yes.

"Ohh fuck," she groans. "Landon."

So tight and clasping.

Her body's like a drug. The more I get, the more I need.

I shove myself into her again and again, so hard that her back slaps against the wall. In and out. In and out. That's it.

More, yeah. Fuck yeah.

"You're hot as fuck," I growl.

Her tight little pussy clasps eagerly against my cock. I fuck her hard and good and rough, until she's shaking, groaning my name as she comes...

I let her calm down a bit after she comes, but not long. I need more of that sweet pussy of hers.

In and out. Fast and faster. More. More. Yeah.

And then I'm coming, she's coming. We're coming.

"That's my girl," I growl, "that's it."

All she can say are pleasured-out syllables that don't make any sense.

Afterwards, I lose track of how long I hold her in my arms. All I know is that it feels damn good.

And then we hear the door open.

CHAPTER 21

Kyra

"Shit!" we sputter, separating.

Luckily, I recognize the dark-haired head looking away in the entrance.

"Sorry," says Greyson.

I wish I could sink to the bottom of this pool and keep sinking.

"Need something?" Landon snaps at him.

"Just thought I'd go explore while Harley was watching Madison. I didn't know - "

"It's fine," Landon grumbles, reaching for his bathing suit. "We should be going anyway."

"Yeah, well..." Greyson's clearly dying of embarrassment, although I'm the one whose heart's beating so franticly that part of me thinks it'll plop right out of my chest and drown itself in protest. "I'll just be going."

"You do that," Landon grumbles.

Once he's gone, Landon and I turn to each other. He's still wearing an irritated scowl, holding his bathing suit as if he isn't quite sure what to do with it. Or maybe he knows and doesn't want to.

Me, I've sunk into the water so it goes up to my chin. If only I could be annoyed instead of embarrassed, like he is.

"Yeah?" he says.

"Kill me now," I say.

"At least it was him," Landon says with a chuckle, giving my thighs a caress. "Although I was wanting to..."

"Landon." I wade away, ignoring the frissons of pleasure. "No. Time for bed."

I've learned my lesson. We were lucky enough not to be caught the first time. No way am I tempting fate by doing it again.

Not sure what offenses they kick you out of Disney World for, but fucking in the hotel hot tub may be one of them.

Getting caught by the brother of the guy I'm seeing isn't exactly an aphrodisiac. At least not to me.

Meanwhile, Landon's face has dropped. He's turned away to get on his bathing suit.

I should do the same. Although it's slippery and ungainly, trying to get the two sopping cotton pieces on while in the water. After stumbling into the bottoms, on the third attempt to tie up my top, I finally give up and ask Landon, "A little help?"

I turn so he can tie up the bikini top, which he does without a word.

The room's quiet, punctuated by the odd trickle of water. It seems eerie now. Oppressive.

The feeling follows us into the pool room, down the hallways, even back into my room. We say goodbye to Harley with a minimum of words, although she's all chatty good humor, and then, once again, it's just us. Eyeing each other.

Why is it even awkward now, anyway? Is he actually that pissed that I turned him down for a second time?

Is that all this is to Landon - just about getting his way with me? No, I'm probably just jumping to sleep-deprived stupid conclusions. Although he isn't saying anything.

"Goodbye, then," I say, with a light wave.

"Bye," he says, no wave.

Back in the too-bright fluorescent-lit bathroom, I try not to look at my wan-faced reflection. I know how crap and uncertain I feel without having to look at it in the face.

What just happened? Why is this relationship such a continual mindfuck?

And after he was so sweet and perfect with me and Maddy...

Something annoying Mom said about rinsing out chlorine from my swimsuit echoes in my head, so I rinse it off and sling it into the shower to dry.

Better not think about it.

**

"Wakey, wakey, Mom!" Maddy trills at some ungodly hour.

My eyelashes flutter a smidgen open, then think better of it. Then the light scorches red brightness through my lids.

Yes, Madison, my dear merciless child, has opened the curtains all the way.

"What time is it?" I manage to groan.

"7:30," she chirps.

"Maddy!" I could've chucked a pillow at her if I felt like moving. "You know it's our vacation."

"We gotta get out there early," Madison says in a firm 'mom' voice that makes me scowl. "Otherwise the lines will be super long."

I just lie there. Maybe if I don't say anything, just lie here and pretend to be asleep, she'll give up and I can -

"Mom?"

I sigh, glaring open my eyes a crack. "Fine. Give me a minute."

I end up needing about fifteen. Five to wrestle myself into a half-upright position, another five to down the coffee Madison so kindly brought me. A final five to change into something more public-appropriate than silly yet awesome sheep PJ bottoms Madison bought for Christmas last year.

"Know what rides you want to go on?" I ask Maddy after I've downed another coffee and feel a little less like walking death.

One bonus is that Madison's so excited that she even dressed herself, complete with a not-terrible ponytail and her way-overpacked backpack.

We'll deal with that later, though. As well as the talk we're going to have about wake-up times if I'm going to survive these next few days. Who knows, maybe I should've splurged for those skip-the-line passes so this wouldn't be a thing. Whatever. Right now, we - I - need food. And lots of it.

After a failed attempt to find the buffet ourselves, we end up just following some hungry-looking family there. It's filled with weary parents and excited kids, and, at a table by the window, with Greyson and Harley, and Landon.

Greyson and Harley are side by side, sharing a mountain of blueberry and strawberry pancakes, while Landon's busy wolfing down a full plate of eggs and bacon. Seeing us, he waves.

"Whoa, where did you get that?" Maddy asks, eyes on his chocolate croissant plate.

Landon points to a far-off station with a pyramid of aesthetically-arranged chocolatey confections. "Over there. Quick, though, they only had two left when I snagged this one."

That's all Maddy needs to zip off with a "Be right back, Mom!"

A smile quirks on Landon's face as he turns to me. "She's independent."

"That she is," I say, more stiffly than I intended.

OK, so it's morning now and last night was last night, but still. It ended off weird.

"Listen," he's saying now, leaning in so only I can hear, "about the other night - "

"It's fine," I interrupt him. Now isn't the time. Or place. "Really."

"No." His hand squeezes mine as he soldiers on. "I was upset. I didn't want the night to end and then you - "

"Ended the night." I exhale. Is it really that simple? It is.

I find myself smiling. "Alright, thanks for explaining."

I can't say that I blame him. A few times, as ridiculous as it is, I've felt a bit resentful for him having to leave earlier than I expected. No one likes to end a good time.

"Yeah?" he's saying now with a small smile.

"Yeah," my own smile says.

Damn it, that smile of his is infectious!

Now there's a mischievous twitch to his lips too, surrounded by their sexy stubble. "Did we just... have our first successful almost-fight?"

I laugh with a shrug. "Don't know - you tell me."

Under the table, he squeezes my hand. "We did."

Looking over my shoulder, he laughs.

I follow his gaze, and my jaw drops when I see what's on Madison's plate.

"Oh no you don't," I tell her, moving to intercept her.

A few steps away from our table, clutching her plate to her chest in a protective stance, Madison stops, eyeing me balefully. "But Mom, there were only five left. I had to make sure everyone got one."

Hands on my hips, I ask, "Oh really?"

She bobs her head. "Really." Picking up the first croissant, she hands it to Harley. Then the next to Greyson.

By this point, we're all chuckling.

An hour or so later, we've got our Disney-ready clothes on and our full-but-not-too-full-and-no-outside-food bags packed.

The day gets off to something of a rocky start, which is mainly my fault.

Who would've figured that the lines would be horrendous at freaking 9:15 AM? Or that the skip-the-line passes would happen to be sold out too?

OK, I might've guessed the second part, but still. That doesn't make it less shitty.

A few hours later, we're roasting under the merciless noontime sun and Madison has actually started nodding off by the statue where we've been waiting for a good half hour, when Landon turns to me, waving two passes. "I don't want to beat a dead horse. But Nolan and Emerson definitely won't be needing these."

"Fine," I snap, grabbing them. "Let's just go."

The rest of the day goes smoother. In the time it took us to almost go on one ride, we manage to go on five and get food. Yes, the rest of the day is a whirlwind: rides, more rides, ketchup-laden French fries, a window-sized white chocolate cookie, even more rides. Madison's face-wide grin is the only thing that remains constant as we hit up Space Mountain, the Pirates of the Caribbean, It's a Small World, the Haunted House...

That, and how damn good Landon is with her. Maybe since he's a giant kid himself: lifting his hands up on the roller coasters, pointing out all the coolest things to check out on the rides themselves.

Or it could be that I'm biased because he's so damn gorgeous. He can make a pair of dark wash Levi's and a red t-shirt look like an Abercrombie and Fitch ad.

Dinner that night is at Be My Guest, the Beauty and the Beast-themed restaurant that is way more elegant than I expected. Hearing the name, I expected a campy, toy-laden ode to the Disney classic. Instead, I got glamor that I'd expect more in some upscale adults-only thousand-dollar-a-night resort.

Cherrywood claw-legged table... Gilt ironwork chair... Vast overhead painting of the night sky... Golden chandeliers glittering with flames... A beaming Mickey-hatted Maddy on one side of me... A grinning Landon on the other...

Is this a fairytale?

Or is it a perfect shimmery bubble - destined to be popped?

Even the waiters have smiles so genuine that they make you want to smile too.

"Would you be having the His and Hers Spousal Special?" our red-head waiter asks me and Landon.

"Oh, we're not..." I begin.

"Yes, they are!" Maddy declares delightedly.

"I'll just have steak," I say firmly.

"Me too," Landon agrees, with a sidelong look at me that could mean anything.

After the waiter has left and Maddy has gone to the bathroom - insisting on going by herself - I turn to Landon. "Sorry about that."

He just chuckles. "Don't be."

Under the table, he squeezes my hand again, and this time he doesn't let it go.

The warmth of his hand goes right through me. It sends a fluttery feeling through me, one that makes me want to tap my toes along to the peppy song the small orchestra's playing in the far corner, or just grin like an idiot at nothing at all.

Maybe this is the 'Disney Magic' they talk about? The one I dismissed as a marketing ploy, or a park goer's hollow praise.

Whatever it is, it's really gone to my head. That, or the $500 bottle of wine Landon insisted on getting us.

It's making me feel like anything is possible. Like Landon is here for good. Like him and me, no matter our differences, can actually work. Like I could tell him right now.

"Landon," I say suddenly.

Because - screw it - I should tell him. Screw playing it safe. He's here now, with us, he's proven himself half a dozen times. Maybe this isn't the right time, but the truth is, there never will be a right time.

"Yeah?" he says.

His phone rings.

I pause.

"It's fine," he says. "Can't be important." His hazel-eyed gaze says, not as important as you.

But when it rings again, I can't. Maybe it can wait for tonight. Soon, at least.

"Check it," I urge him, and he does.

Frowning, he's about to reject the call when he glances at the caller ID. His face drops and he picks up. "Hey. What's up?"

A few words from whoever's on the other end, and his scowl deepens.

He gets up, walks off, still talking, his forgotten water still clenched in his hand.

Clearly, he's just found out something bad.

Really bad.

CHAPTER 22

Landon

"We lost the case," Dirk says over the phone. "I'm sorry, Landon." I can hear him shuffling papers in the background. Part of me wants to punch him, to yell.

Or even just laugh.

It feels impossible, getting this news in this place right now. There's too many happy people at pretty tables. Things have been going too well lately.

Fuck.

"Just like that?" I say. "What about the trial?"

"Their key witness finally came forward," Dirk says, with a tone of shrugged shoulders. Remind me to get Storm Inc. a new fucking lawyer. In fact, I know just the one. "She was a bit reluctant to come forward before, naturally. But she's admitted to it all now. She accepted a bribe for the idea, and she has the documents to prove it. Her testimony will sink our case."

This is the kind of thing I'd expect fucking Nolan to say, not our fucking lawyer.

"Come on," I growl, "she can't be cross-examined? Isn't it your job to sink anything they try throwing at us?"

"It is," Dirk admits. More paper shuffling. "But I'm telling you my professional opinion on this. I can try fighting this with everything we have - but we don't have much. And besides, there's another option, a really good one: Goldtree is offering Storm Inc. a sweet deal. I don't know why, the way I figure it they could get a hell of a lot more out of us, but it's what they're asking. I suggest you take it."

Just like that. One minute everything is OK, we've still got a chance, and the next we don't. Not that the case was going well, per se, but hell, I didn't expect it to turn around like this.

Fucking Dad. Look at the mess you've gotten us in.

I can almost see him now. He'd be leaning on one of these golden gilt pillars with enough bravura to get us through any legal fuck-up.

"What's the deal?" I ask Dirk.

No matter what it is, my brothers won't like it. Fuck, I don't like it myself.

"You pay them a couple of million to shut up and go away, and they will," Dirk says, in the same tone as you use to tell someone they won the lottery. "That's it. It's a damn good deal."

Guess in a way we are winning the lottery with what they're asking.

Especially considering the money our Storm TV show is raking in, it's the best deal we could've hoped for. What's the catch?

"That's it?" I say.

"That's it," he says.

Or so they say.

I'll need to think on this. A lot. Talk to my brothers.

"And the witness?" I ask.

When he tells me the name, I slam the cup of water I hadn't realized I'd taken with me down on a gold-inlaid table. "No way. Can't be."

"I saw the video interview with her myself," Dirk says, his tone going curious. "You know her?"

I press my lips together. No point in telling Dirk shit.

"Want me to tell them we'll take it?" Dirk says, perking up.

I'm starting to wonder whose side he's on. Then again, if we fought this, Dirk would get hundreds more billable hours.

I shake my head, even though he can't see it. "Need to talk to my brothers first."

"Alright," he says. "Give me a call. Sorry for bothering you on your vacation."

"Yeah, well. No avoiding it. Thanks, Dirk."

I hang up, unsure of what I'm thanking him for. It was just something Dad did and was good at. He claimed people liked it - thank-you's, I'm sorry's - even if there isn't a real need. It's seemed to check out. Though I forget most times.

I'm still standing where I wandered, staring at nothing. Brain buzzing. Eyes narrowed.

A dumb kid part of me feels like if I stay here, don't go back, maybe I can make it not have happened.

But it did happen. It's over. The trial is over. We lost.

Not officially, not yet.

Sure, I'll talk to my brothers. But they'll all agree. That deal's too sweet to pass up.

No use in fighting a losing battle.

And Kyra?

I need to tell her. Now.

I pick up my cup.

Back at the table, everyone's doing a good job of pretending to be more interested in their meals, minus Madison, who actually is.

Halfway through her Italian wedding soup, she's got a soupy red mustache on her upper lip.

"What's up?" Greyson asks me as I sit down.

The satin-padded chair wants to guide me into a comfortable, half-sprawling position. I don't let it. I need to be sitting upright to say this.

"We lost the case," I say.

Silence, though not really. Families at other tables laugh and chat noisily. Waiters patiently explain menu choices. The mini-orchestra in the corner trills away some tune that sounds familiar and cloying.

Wine glass frozen in hand, halfway to his lips, Greyson stares at me. "What?"

"That was Dirk." I take a long swig of mine. God knows I need it. "Apparently, Goldtree has a star witness who just came forward admitting to the plagiarism. She's got proof too, proof that'll sink us. Dirk recommends we take their offer. They only want a few million."

"What the hell," Greyson grumbles, finally drinking his, then glaring at it, as if it's to blame. "Who?"

"That's what I'd like to know," Kyra says, frowning. Yet her eyes are too wide to be annoyed. Who knows what she's thinking.

"Maybe we should talk..." I begin, reaching for her hand.

Out of all the ways Kyra would want to be told, this can't be one of them.

"No," she says, avoiding my hand with a firm shake of her head. "Tell me."

"Kyra," I say, "you really should - "

"Tell me," she says.

"I don't think - "

"Tell me," she insists.

"Fine," I snap. If she wants to find out like this - all at once in front of everyone, then fine. "It's Pamela."

Her eyebrows leap, then she stares at me, the expression of someone still waiting for the answer. "Not funny."

Madison finally looks up from her soup, some of it slopping out of her spoon back into the bowl. "Did Pompom do something wrong, Mom?"

"No, she didn't," Kyra says firmly. "It's just some..." She looks to me.

All their eyes are on me, expectant. I look away. "Sorry, Kyra."

"No," she snaps, face dropping with every word, "that's not possible. She would've told me. She... she would've known, my case..." She trails off, getting out her phone and rising, abruptly stopping to wheel around to throw an unconvincing smile at Madison. "Sorry, I... Maddy, you OK to wait here with the others?"

Back at her soup, Madison just nods her dark-haired head with a slurpy sip. "Sure, Mom."

"Damn, that's awful," Harley comments, watching Kyra walk outside to make the call. "She and this Pamela are close?"

"Best friends for years," I say quietly, clenching the edge of the table.

"This case," Harley says, shaking her head.

'This case' is right. This can't look good for Kyra, who unknowingly had the witness they needed right under her nose.

Kyra comes back salt-white, with her eyebrows halfway up her face. "She admitted it. Wants to talk when I get back."

She half-sits half-falls into her chair. "I can't believe it."

Madison's looking up from her soup again. "What did Pompom do?"

"I..." Kyra shakes her head wearily. "She kept something from me. Something important. I'll explain when we get home."

My hand seeks out hers. But when I grab it, it's as cold and lifeless as a dead fish.

"I had no idea either," I tell her.

She has to know that. This is as much a blow to me as it is to her.

"I know," she says, though she isn't looking at me. Her fingers are around her small, rose-engraved spoon, turning and turning it. "Just... Goldtree making an offer to your lawyer like that, without consulting me at all? That can't be good. I tried calling them, but..."

Ring... ring... ring...

She snatches up her phone. "That's them. Sorry. Be right back." She hurries off.

I sit there, trying to eat the steak I have no appetite for.

Funny how much can change over a few minutes. Now, the music is headache-inducing. The people annoying. The decor over-the-top.

Fuck this. Fuck it all.

Kyra comes back a few minutes later, looking even worse than before. "That was them."

"And?" I ask.

Her mouth twists around the words. "And they want to see me ASAP. Tomorrow." Her eyes fill and she quickly dabs away the oncoming tears with a long exhale.

My arms go around her and she sinks into them mechanically.

I gape at her, my mind churning round and round.

What the hell do I do now? How do I make this better?

"Do we have to go home?" Madison's soup is done, her eyes hazel saucers on Kyra. The Mickey Mouse ears are akimbo, so much so that they're almost off her head.

"No," Kyra says firmly, straightening herself out of my arms. "Work wants to see me... But I'm not going to let them ruin this for us. You're the most important thing in the world to me."

"She can stay with us," I find myself offering.

Somehow, the idea of watching someone else's kid doesn't seem as awful as it normally would. Even today, while I was a bit nervous, it actually went great. And not even just because I was trying to impress Kyra. I genuinely like Madison. She's fun.

But Kyra's already shaking her head. "I can't ask you to do that."

"Of course you can!" Harley urges her, with a toss of her sandy blonde head, gap-toothed smile sympathetic and eager. "We love Maddy, and I'd hate for her to miss out. Though if you don't feel comfortable..."

Eyes closed, Kyra rubs at her temples, exhaling long and ragged. "No. Yeah. You know what? It can work. My mom's in town anyway."

Huh. Mrs. Masterson was my greatest fan before. But now...

"Oh?" I say.

"There's this book convention thing this weekend," Kyra recounts quickly, with a vague and unconvincing smile. "She doesn't even like going, but this old friend always forces her to, so she'll probably be happy to have an excuse to skip it. I didn't even think about it, but... yeah." She bobs her head weakly, gaze going to Madison. "That OK, honey? If you see the rest of the park with Grandma? Mom just has this work thing and..."

Madison's lower lip is stuck out, her forehead creased in thought. Weird, how damn familiar she seems. Then again, she is Kyra's daughter.

Finally, with one solemn nod, Madison says, "It's OK."

Kyra goes over to give her a hug, smoothing her hair and straightening her Mickey ears. "I'm so sorry, honey. I promise I'll make it up to you."

"It's OK, Mom," Madison says, smiling. "But if you made me leave Disney World early too, then you'd have some major making up to do."

Kyra just chuckles. "Don't I know it." Rising, she gets out her phone. "I'll call my mom, and as soon as she gets here, I should go... See what flight I can catch. If any."

I get out my phone. "I'll start looking at what's out there now while you call your mom."

"OK." She's too rushed to argue, has already dialed the number.

For the next few minutes, we pick at the rest of our meals while Kyra calls up her mom and I get her a flight back to New York for tonight. Afterwards, we kill time watching some cartoon featuring two fat cats before her mom finally meets us at the hotel, her silver-haired head wearing a great big smile as she gives Madison, then Kyra a hug - "My darlings." As they part, she whirls around and gapes at me. "You."

Shit. I hadn't wanted to meet Kyra's mom like this.

Yeah, judging by that horrified frown, she definitely isn't my greatest fan now. Not that I blame her.

"Well." She recovers herself well, turning her body and gaze to Maddy, as though she could make me disappear from sheer ignoring alone. Wonder-fucking-ful. "It's time you were getting to bed, young lady."

"Grandma," Madison groans. "It's only nine."

"A whole hour past your bedtime," Mrs. Masterson returns immediately with a winning smile.

We say our goodbyes, hugs for all - except that Mrs. Masterson is still determinedly ignoring me - and then Kyra pulls away with a final wave, already eyeing the doors with a determined scowl. "Time for me to get going too."

"Me too," I tell her.

"It's fine," she says.

"I booked myself a seat too," I explain. I couldn't just let her go alone like this. I need to be there for her. "I didn't tell you in the rush of everything."

"Oh," she says, the sound more a sigh than a real word. Then, she shrugs and we head out together. Clearly, she's had enough for today.

The pasty white taxi driver with a handlebar mustache putters along below the speed limit infuriatingly. I have to physically restrain myself from throwing him out of the car when he feigns deafness to my stiff requests for him to go faster.

Finally, though, we get there. The sprawling airy building filled with hulking palm trees. Orlando International Airport. We even make it on our red-eye flight with a few minutes to spare.

I put on some headphones and listen to some Radiohead so I won't think about it. How Kyra's staring at everything without seeing it. How she didn't even notice the few times I tried holding her hand.

This isn't about me, us, though. Being a lawyer was her dream. Now, by the sound of it, that dream may be in danger.

I clench at the arm rest, the bar between us. Although there's a whole lot more between us right now.

This is one instance where I can't help. At all.

Other than giving her space.

The rest of the flight, she stays sleeping, and I keep listening. I have some of those free pretzels. I'd have gotten us first-class seats, but they were all booked up. This is getting us where we're going anyway.

Once we've retrieved our luggage and made it to the taxis, we pause.

"Thank you for everything," Kyra says, half-turned to me, half-turned to the taxis. Her sad brown eyes meet mine. "Sorry I had to leave like this"

"Don't be," I say, with a shake of my head. "I'm sorry I picked up that fucking phone."

Kyra's shoulders rise in a semi-shrug. "We had to find out sometime."

She's right, of course. But if it could've waited even another day... a half-day. Just so we could've had some more time...

"Do you want me to come with you?" I say. "I could..."

I trail off; she's shaking her head already.

"I need to do this alone," she says, body and gaze swiveled to her destination now. "I'm sorry."

I don't mention how she's saying that a lot lately. I don't urge her to let me come along. I don't take her hand.

Even though I can't remember wanting anything this much.

"I'll let you go," I say.

"OK," she says.

And, fuck me, she looks so pretty in her shimmering black dress. The one from the dinner she never had time to change out of.

I should tell her.

Tell her that fuck it, whatever it is, we'll make it work. That I want to be there for her, with her.

But all I do is say "OK" and let her leave in her taxi, and go home in mine.

The cab ride home takes too long. The driver isn't slow this time; it just does.

Back at my place, I go up the elevator, down the hallway.

Then I open up the door to my penthouse, and gape at what I see. "What the... fuck."

CHAPTER 23

Kyra

This is it.

The day. The hour.

Last night after I got home from the airport, I couldn't sleep because of it. Now, I can hardly breathe because of it.

Best navy-and-grey Hugo suit and I'm-not-afraid smile on, two coffees in my belly, I'm ready. Outside the door of their office, waiting with a dismal looking dracaena, I try to remember to breathe.

What are you waiting for? Knock. Do it. Get this over with.

It's 8:45 AM, fifteen minutes earlier than specified. But that's the kind of woman I am, the kind of lawyer I am - the kind who shows up early and goes above and beyond for every case. Who drills at it until it's won.

Then why am I nervous as hell? Why can't I knock on this goddamn stupid fake wood door to Goldtree's goddamn stupid ugly office?

Probably because the woman who goes above and beyond, who roots out everything to know about a case and throws it in the face of the opposition like acid, who pecks and pecks at a case like a woodpecker, has failed. Big time.

For the first time, I'm not sure I can argue that I killed this case. I'm not sure I can vouch for myself.

Screw it -

My knuckles connect with the door harder than I intended. The impact jars up my arm.

The door opens. I swallow.

Some fake fruit air freshener scent assaults me as I take in the scene.

Every chair is occupied - every who's-who executive is in attendance.

This is so not good.

"Ms. Masterson, do come in," Bart says.

As he moves aside, the bright overhead lights shine on his bald spot. He goes to sit down with everyone else.

There's no chair for me.

"We'll cut to the chase," he says pleasantly. "You're off the case."

"I will too, then." My voice comes out shockingly cool; I'm all nerves inside. "Why?"

He peers at me a bit froggily. "Don't you know? Well, here it is: You missed key information, due, we believe, to your closeness to our employee in question who has admitted to accepting the bribe. Pamela Thorson came forward herself. Then, it's come to our attention that you've been involved with the defendant's President, Mr. Landon Storm."

There it is. What I've been dreading. What I need to lie about. What I'm not willing to lie about.

"So, that's it, then." Somehow, a weight has settled in my chest - and been lifted. It probably hasn't sunk in yet. "Even though we were winning the case anyway."

"Winning - hadn't won." Bart's glare is cool. "Who knows how much time or legal fees we would've saved if it hadn't been for you.

As it is, we just want this all wrapped up as quickly as possible. We have a business to run."

I find myself nodding, turning away. "I understand."

As I walk out, behind me I hear, "Goodbye, Ms. Masterson."

I head for the elevator, head held high, face forced calm. Bart didn't say the rest, of course. Why would he?

But that doesn't make it not so. That this isn't as simple as being thrown off a case. This story, this debacle will follow me. For months, years, maybe even longer than that.

I'm not going to be able to just walk away from this.

Then there's the timing of it. Jackson and Peterson, my firm, their annual review is in another week or so. An annual review where Cindy specifically mentioned the possibility of letting some people go. Yes, the worst goddamn timing possible.

Shit.

I drive home, feeling like I'm floating all the way. Not a good kind of floating, though. The kind of floating of a bubble popped - the kind of floating seconds before the fall. The only question is: when will the fall come?

Back at my place, Landon's waiting by the front door looking sheepish yet painfully handsome.

"Sorry," he says. "I know I should've called, but..."

"It's OK," I find myself saying as droplets splatter onto my exposed hand as I open the door.

It's started raining at some point. Oh.

Inside, my purse slops to the floor and I go to the couch to sit down.

"I'm sorry," I say to Landon, with an attempt at a smile. "I won't be much company right now. It might be best..."

"Oh no, you aren't getting rid of me that easily," he says firmly, coming to sit beside me. If this was any other time, the feel of his strong, warm leg beside me would be reassuring. But it's not any other time.

"So," he says.

"I lost the case," I say. "Worst possible time, too. My firm's all set for their annual review and they're letting people go."

"Jesus, Kyra."

"I know."

Landon never was good at comforting me, which is why I'm surprised when his fingers entwine with mine, lift them to his lips. "What do you need? We could hire you for Storm. Dirk has been underperforming lately."

I gape at him.

"What?" he says.

"Is that what you think I want?" I ask incredulously. "Some kind of pity job thrown my way?"

"No." He scowls. "Just trying to help. Storm Inc. is a big client. It could look good at this annual review."

"What, that the guy I'm dating and lost a case over decided to toss me a job?"

His hand drops mine as his eyes narrow. "That why you lost it?"

"That's what they said." I try to keep the bitterness out of my voice, but I can't manage it. This is too messed up. "That and the Pamela thing. That I was too personally involved and missed key things." My arms wrap around myself as a ragged sob falls out of me. Now, it's hitting me. Great. "I can't do this right now, Landon."

His hand lifts to me, wavers. "I keep saying the wrong thing. I don't know what to do."

The earnest pain in his voice makes me look up. His face has it too.

"There's nothing you can do," I say sadly, taking his hand myself. "Anyway, it's not you, it's me. I'm the one who keeps making mistakes. Mistake after fucking mistake."

"What are you saying?" he asks, light brown eyebrows drawn together.

"I'm saying that, ever since I've started seeing you again, it feels like my head isn't on straight. Like I keep making missteps."

"Things haven't been a fucking walk in the park for me either," Landon growls. "I'm still here."

"But maybe you shouldn't be," I say sadly. "Maybe all this fighting and trying and struggling... maybe it's too much. Maybe the cost is too high."

Landon lets my hand drop. "You don't think this is worth fighting for?"

"I don't know. Do you?"

His response is immediate and sure. "Yeah, I sure as hell do. What the hell, Kyra?"

"Maybe this can work," I say slowly, still not daring to look at him. I know those hazel eyes of his would diminish the little self-control I have left. "But right now... I think I need some time. This is a lot to take in at once, and I need to be on my A game for that annual review. Need my head clear."

"Kyra - "

"I'm sorry, Landon."

"Don't be sorry," he urges me, clasping at both my hands. "Don't do this."

I still can't look at him. "I'm not sure I have a choice anymore."

Quiet. Except for the static of the TV. God, Landon smells good.

"I just... I can't get this uncertainty out of my head," I confess, pulling my hands away. "That you'll run out on me when I need you most. I know it's stupid, holding onto what happened before, but I can't seem to let it go, no matter how I try. I can't have that in the back of my head while I'm dealing with all this. I just can't. I'm sorry." Now, I finally dare to look him in the face.

There's an odd look there, one I don't recognize. Not anger. Not sadness. Not fear or nervousness.

"I never told you," he's saying now, "why I dumped you all those years ago."

Something twists in me.

"Don't," I say hoarsely, pulling away.

He catches my hand again. "Just hear me out, Kyra, please."

I rise, suddenly mad. Mad at this whole stupid situation. Mad at him, still making demands of me when he's the last person who should be. "No. No, I won't. You didn't give me any explanation then, why the hell should I stick around and let you make one now? And you didn't just 'dump' me, Landon. You dumped me with no warning, no explanation, at the biggest party of the year in front of all of our closest friends. And then you ghosted me. And now, you show up here and - "

"Hear me out," Landon says, and now I recognize the hurt on his face. "Just - listen to what I have to say, and if you want to kick me out after, then you can, alright?"

"I've heard that offer before."

"And I mean it," he says simply. "Please."

When I don't say anything, he starts talking. "Before I met you, I never told you, but I wasn't doing great in school. Too much partying. It was completely my fault. Dad decided to cut me off. Made me pay my own way - which was fair, considering all his money I had wasted on failed courses. The term I met you, if I'd failed it, I would've had to work years to afford just another semester. I couldn't afford to fail."

He swallows, runs a hand through his light brown hair. He doesn't seem to want to look at me for some reason. Not that I'm dying to lock eyes right now anyway. Screw what he says. Screw his reasons. Nothing can explain away what he did.

"But I couldn't concentrate when I was with you," he continues. "Or when I was without you. It messed up my head. I couldn't study, I couldn't do anything right. I flunked my one course, and knew I couldn't afford to screw up even just one more. And with that jerk friend of yours... it wasn't right, but I ended things because of that. I didn't want to explain or face you because I knew I'd cave. I knew I'd end up confessing it all to you, telling you that you were the girl I saw myself marrying... Then, the next year, when I was finally out of school and I tried to reach out... nothing. You wouldn't take my calls, my texts, nothing."

Finally, Landon looks to me. All I can do is blink back. It takes me a good few seconds to realize that he's waiting for an answer.

"I had you blocked," I say, glaring at him. "I wasn't going to sit around waiting for you to reach out forever."

He shrugs. "I don't blame you."

"Good."

"Good."

We sit there.

So, that's it then. That's the explanation. Did he mean it? Does it matter?

Too much has happened. God knows what I actually think.

"I get it," he's saying now, quietly, emphatically. "I screwed up, OK? I don't plan on making the same mistake twice."

I swallow.

He's waiting for a response. One I don't want to give.

"It might not be up to you," I finally say quietly.

We sit there for another minute. Two. Three. He rises. "So, you want me to go."

I rise. "I don't want you to." I swallow. Don't look at him - don't let the pain in those hazel eyes convince you, sway you. Don't let who this man is now change your mind about what he did when he was a cruel boy. "But I think you should."

"OK," he says, not moving.

"OK," I say.

He goes to the door. It's still raining out there.

"Goodbye," he says, pausing to search for my face. Probably for any signs of wavering, anything he can use to justify staying.

But I keep mine lawyer-cool.

It's not at all how I'm feeling. But it's convincing enough to make him leave when I say, "Goodbye."

I go back to sit on the couch.

I don't pick up my phone. Even though I'll have to see Pamela at some point. Talk things over, if they even can be. I don't want to think of that right now.

I don't want to think of anything right now.

A knock at the back door has me rushing there. He wouldn't dare - he -

Of course he would.

It's Landon, of course, standing there in the pouring rain, smiling miserably when I open the door.

"I'm sorry," he yells over the deluge. "But I can't just let this go. I want you in my life, Kyra. I don't care what it takes. I don't care what you need from me - time, more trips, babysitting, whatever it takes. I need you in my life - whatever it takes."

"I..." I start and trail off.

Why is it that what I want to say and should say are never the same?

I step outside into the rain. To tell him no, I'm sorry, but I need time.

The rain splatters coolly on me, though I hardly notice.

I open my mouth to tell him, and his sweeps to mine in answer. And, as they move together, I find that's the real answer I've been wanting to give all this time.

The cool rain drills out any thought from my head. That and his lips, guiding mine, reassuring mine.

This man, this wildly gorgeous man...

Our fingers entwine, run along each other's bodies.

He's here. Here for me, and what he said...

It doesn't make it alright, what he did. But it's damn near close.

"I'm sorry," he kisses into my ear. "I made the worst mistake of my life. I'm sorry."

And then we kiss some more. We kiss ourselves outside further, onto the grass, him on top of me, me on top of him, the rain on top of both of us. We kiss our clothes off.

It should be cold, out here in the grass-scented rain. But when I'm with him, it's only warm.

We kiss him inside of me. Slow and steady and building. Warm and warming. Tingling overtakes me. Until the rain and I are battling to see who can be louder.

Afterwards, he holds me. Then the kissing starts again, the building. Him and me. Him inside me. Us. As one.

In and out, deep and deeper. Until we're crying out together. Coming together. Shaking together.

Then, later, holding each other. When I turn to look at him, though, he won't meet my eye.

"What is it?" I ask him.

The rain's tapered off; now it's just a sad drizzle.

"Forget it," he finally says.

"Landon."

"Fine," he says, scowling. "I'll tell you."

CHAPTER 24

Kyra

He glares into the rain, strokes along my arm absent-mindedly, and just when I'm about to urge him again, he says, "I love you."

Just like that. In the casual tone of 'I brushed my teeth'. In the resentful tone of 'You owe me $400 and it's been months'.

I love you - I love you - I love love love love love you.

I gape at him.

Is the drizzle muddling my hearing? Is my own overeager brain putting the words I want to hear in his mouth?

"Forget it," he says, turning away.

"No," I reply, turning his face back to me, his stubble scratching my fingertips. "You mean it?"

A half-shrug. "Maybe."

I grin. "Maybe?"

He said it, now it's your turn, a quiet voice urges me.

As if it's as easy as that: I love you - hey, I love you - guess what, me too, I really do, love you.

Hell no. It's not as easy as that. It's fucking hard.

Even with his face inches away from mine, his familiar deep brow, strong nose, wide-set hazel eyes and endlessly kissable lips, he seems like he's still turned away.

I shouldn't say it, what I'm feeling. It's a bad idea. A terrifying one.

But the rain's made everything slippery and I can't seem to hold onto it how I should.

"I love you too," I breathe, and his eyes come alive.

"You mean it?"

I just laugh, and that's answer enough for him.

His lips sweep to mine, my jawline. "Kyra."

"Landon," I murmur back.

He wraps his arms around me, beaming like a kid on Halloween. "That's it, then."

With him smiling like that, how can I not smile too? "What's it?"

That grin. "We are."

"We'll see about that," I say, although my smile is a dead giveaway.

Not that I'm so sure. There's still...

Shit.

How can I still keep that from Landon now?

I need to tell him, and soon. Should have already told him, really. But right now, I have way too much on my plate as it is, with my work and the whole Pamela situation.

If Landon were to react badly to it...

No.

I'll tell him soon. Soon, but not yet.

"What's up?" he asks now.

"I... still have to talk to Pamela," I confess.

"Oh. Now?"

"I want to get it over with," I say.

Which is true, but what's truer is that what just happened between us terrifies me and I want to be alone. And call Pamela at some point. Having my head screwed on properly would be nice too.

"Makes sense." He nods, putting on his clothes, all casual. As if what just happened didn't. "I'll leave you to it, then."

Did what just happened not happen? Did he really say it?

He's walking away when I stop him. "Landon - wait."

He pauses, with a look like he could still smile. "Yeah?"

"Say it again."

His brow creases with incomprehension.

"The L word," I say, feeling my cheeks heating up.

God, I feel like a teenage girl, doing 'Does He Like Me' quizzes in J14.

He squints, with the beginnings of a smirk, but now I know it's all for show. "Not sure I know that one."

"Say it!" I demand.

A full smirk. "Say what?"

"Landon!"

He chuckles. "Fine." Heads off. He's almost out of sight when, with a wave, he calls over his shoulder, "Love you!"

It travels all through me, his 'love you'. Warms me. Keeps me smiling all the way back to the couch.

There, I laze amidst the lint (mental note: finally get around to cleaning this thing), even wash the single dish I've used since I got back. Then, I change a handful of times before I find a pair of black velvet sweats that are grungy but not too grungy. I'm not about to dress up for a best friend who stabbed me in the back.

Until, finally, I can't put it off anymore. I text her.

Can you come over?

- Sure. Now? she replies immediately.

Now, I reply, going back to sink on the couch and scowl at nothing in particular except what's about to happen.

There. It's done.

Ding-dang-dong-ding, the doorbell goes, far too soon.

I sit there until it's donged itself out. Until I can think of absolutely nothing else keeping me on this sink-seated couch other than fear.

Even if it does make sense. Pompom's my best friend. What if this ends it all?

I rise, steeling myself.

Whatever happens today, whatever I find out, I have to know the truth.

"Hey," she says, standing there, her pink glossed mouth moving with what could be an attempt at a smile.

I glare at her flatly, my eyes doing an impressed once-over of her.

Who dares to get all spruced up - pink gloss, winged liner - when they're coming to their best friend to beg forgiveness? If she is even here for that.

"Hey," I say, stepping aside so she can come in.

"It's OK," she says, not moving. She's wearing her polka-dot wash blue jeans and tight tie-dye crop top. Definitely not 'I'm sorry' wear. "If you don't want..." She trails off, then bursts out, "I'm so sorry, Ky."

I stare at her for a long minute, then, finally, ask, "Why?"

Why she basically stabbed a knife into my back, not why she's sorry. We both know why she's sorry. What she did.

As for me, looking at her, even with the new sheen of tears in her green eyes, I feel zero sympathy. Her sleek straightened red hair and well-rested look isn't helping. Not that I expected her to show up looking like a domestic abuse insomniac, but still. "I just don't understand it."

I open the door further and gesture her inside. We go to the kitchen together.

"I wanted to tell you," Pamela admits, twining a strand of hair round her finger, round and round and round as she stands in the middle of the room looking lost, "but my job was on the line..." Sad chuckle. "Now I lost it anyway, of course. I knew it was a bad idea accepting that bribe to hand over the idea, but it was a bad year. My dad needed that big operation and I needed the money to help him. Colin was so persuasive and I thought..." She shakes her head. "Thought I could keep it under wraps. But the guilt kept eating away at me. And when my dad found out a few days ago, he demanded I come forward. So, I did."

"But why didn't you come to me, is what I can't understand," I say, wanting to shake her. 'So, I did' - does she have any fucking clue what her 'so, I did' is going to cost me? "Don't you realize - "

"I wasn't thinking straight," Pamela confesses, whipping the hair back. "I'd just lived with it for so long, I just wanted it off my chest. Blurt it out. I didn't think it through. I just reacted. I was afraid that if I didn't come forward, I'd keep making excuses."

What she's saying makes sense, would make sense, except -

"I'm the lawyer on the case," I snarl. "You didn't think - "

"No," she says miserably, an up-down of her shoulders. "I didn't."

Her gaze searches mine. "But Goldtree, they didn't actually..."

"They did," I confirm with a swift nod. "I'm off the case."

"Oh," is all she says, sagging against the kitchen counter behind her. "Shit."

"Yeah, basically." I let out a laugh, though there's no mirth in it. "The firm's having its annual review this week, too."

Pamela's mouth forms a horrified 'O' in comprehension. "Kyra, I never thought - "

"Yeah, that's just it." My voice is rising and it feels good, good to be letting this anger out. "You never thought about anything other than yourself. And now I could lose my job."

Her head is hung, looking at the tile floor we put down together, way back when I first bought this place.

Pamela's been with me through everything. But this... this could ruin everything. Has it?

"I don't know what to say," she says quietly, meeting my gaze miserably. "I'm sorry. I know it doesn't mean much." Sad, bitter laugh. "Hell, it means jack shit. "But I never wanted for any of this to happen."

"Why couldn't you have asked me for help for your dad's operation?" I ask. I still can't get my head around all this. That it was Pamela. Pompom. That she was the one who took the bribe from Collin Storm. She was the one who could've handed me the case tied in a bow. And instead turned the bow into a noose around my neck. "You know I would've been happy to."

"I know, I just..." A sigh. "You know how my family is about borrowing money. My mom has never been able to pay back my uncle for that money he gave them for the house, so we try to avoid borrowing at all costs. I didn't want the money I'd borrowed from you hanging over our heads and messing up our friendship if I couldn't pay it back." She exhales, grabs a tissue from the countertop and blows her nose noisily. When she looks up, her nose is pink on the freckled tip, her eyes rimmed with red. "But now I've messed it up anyway, haven't I?"

The question hangs in the air. It sits me down on the kitchen chair, opens and closes my mouth.

How to begin to answer that?

One thing is for sure: I won't be able to do it justice now, with how I'm feeling. Like I've run a marathon. I guess it isn't all that surprising, with all that's happened in the past 24 hours. Talk about emotional exhaustion.

"Sorry for messing up your vacation too, for what it's worth," Pamela's saying now. "If there's anything I can do..." She trails off, stepping away from the counter and drawing herself upright.

She lets out a long, ragged breath, presses her lips together. Her green eyes are bright with tears. "You need time. I get it." Head bob. "I just hope you can forgive me at some point."

She turns away, pausing. Waiting for me to say something that I can't. Promise that things will be OK.

But I don't know that. I don't know what tomorrow will bring.

All I know is that right now, I want to hug her. And slap her. Yell at her and cry with her.

"Goodbye, Pompom," I say softly.

A half-smile crosses her face. Maybe she's right - maybe there's some hope in that. That I can even still bear to call her that.

"Goodbye, Kyky," she says, leaving.

A glance at my phone finds that it's almost noon. Mom and Maddy will be back around seven tonight. That's when I'll have to sit Madison down and tell her.

I have a long day ahead of me.

**

When Madison comes home, she's sunburnt, sleepy and delighted silly from her trip, trying to tell me about five things at once. I get her some KD, and Mom recounts the rides they went on, the food and fun they had, but I only half-hear her. My mind's on the task at hand. What I have to do once Mom leaves. She already knows what I have to tell my daughter, anyway.

Sitting on Maddy's bed after I've read her Babar book a little over an hour later, I know it's far from the best time to tell her. Even half-asleep as she is, she's radiating happiness, still riding high from the Disney trip.

There'd be a lot of better times to tell her than now. But I've been putting this off for too long. Years too long.

She deserves to know.

Afterwards, she cries and yells and barricades herself in her room. But before half an hour is up, she's turned off the Avril Lavigne and I can hear soft snores coming from her room.

I'm nodding off on the couch, half-scrolling through job postings online, when a call wakes me.

"Hey," Landon says.

"Hey," I say.

And then I say the rest of it. "Can you come over? There's something I should tell you."

Although I don't say all of it: It's something I should've told you years ago.

CHAPTER 25

Landon

What can it be?

The question plagues me as I get into my burrito-smelling car. As I toss aside the wrapper from my recent takeout, I scowl.

My head's still reeling from that model Nolan let into my place. His version of a 'present'. Of course I told her to fuck off, booted her out. I really need to talk to that guy. And take back my keys.

Anyway, now I'm headed back to Kyra's, for whatever she has to say.

There's no point in trying to guess at it; that woman is about as predictable as the weather. Maybe even less.

Just when I think I know where we stand... boom. She wants nothing to do with me. Or, whoops, she has a kid. A kid who's actually pretty cool, but still.

No sooner have I knocked on her front door, then it's opening. Almost like she was standing right by it waiting.

What can it be?

She sits me on the couch and then she starts talking, words all odd and prepared-sounding, like she memorized cue cards for this.

"So," she says with a nod, "remember how when we were in college and I had that pregnancy scare you started freaking out, looking up abortion clinics?"

No fucking way.

"Hold up," I say, trying to keep my voice calm. "Are you pregnant?"

"No," she says, a smile that isn't as relieved as it should be.

"Then what's the problem?" I ask.

As far as I'm concerned, any day you don't find out about an accidental pregnancy is a good day. And Kyra looks nervous and wired as hell.

"Can you let me finish?" she snaps.

I shrug. "Sure."

"And remember how you were vehemently against having kids?" she continues.

Why do I feel like this is leading somewhere weird?

"Kyra." I frown at her. Maybe I wasn't a star dude when I was younger, but she doesn't have to keep throwing my doucheness in my face. "We were in our early 20s, and I didn't even have a decent job."

"Yeah, but..." Kyra trails off.

I never been some kind of emotional magician, but is that guilt on her face?

"You said you didn't want kids, period," Kyra reminds me, crossing her arms over her chest. She's changed into something comfortable looking... but still sexy. "We almost broke up over it a few times."

"Yeah, well."

"Yeah, well, what?"

I shrug. "The only experience I had of kids was my cousins, little demons who lit our Storm extended family cabin on fire because they weren't allowed to play Game Boy one afternoon."

"OK," Kyra says hesitantly, "But now?"

I stare at her.

No way can she be getting at what it seems like she is. No fucking way.

I rise. "Why are you asking me all this? One second you don't think we should be together, the next you're trying to discuss kids with me?"

"That's not what I'm trying to do," she says quietly, looking to the wall.

"Then what are you trying to do?" I find myself snapping, storming over in front of her. "Because I'm fucking baffled. And the way you called me to come over like this was some goddamn emergency..."

I'm tired of this 20 questions game. I want to know what the fuck is up. Now.

She rises, then sits down again in a single exhale. "I'm... trying to make sure this is the right thing." She looks at me sadly. "You never pushed it on asking me who Madison's father was."

"I wanted to know." I shrug. "You didn't want to tell me."

"Yeah, well." Her lower jaw trembles. Her whole body starts doing it too. What the hell can be this bad? Is the father someone I know? "I don't know how to say this, but she's yours."

My head jerks her way. "What?"

No fucking way.

She stands up again, starts pacing, eyes fixed determinedly ahead. "I know, it's just - the way you broke up with me. And how against kids you were. I didn't want Madison having a father like that. I didn't want you to be in her life just out of some twisted sense of obligation, not even wanting to."

"You're saying - " I snarl, standing in front of her so she has to stop. Has to look at me. "You're saying that... all this time... all these fucking years... I had a daughter? We have a daughter? Madison is my..."

I trail off, falling onto the couch.

Jesus fucking Christ. No wonder she seemed so familiar. No wonder we got along so well.

Holy fuck.

By now, Kyra's paced herself to a corner, peering over her shoulder at me like she's afraid to. "I'm so, so, so sorry, Landon. I understand if... after this... you don't want to - "

"Don't presume that you know what I want," I snap, getting up and sitting back down again. "You've been doing that this whole fucking time and look at where that's got us. Jesus, Kyra, I missed years of her life. Years. Does Madison know?"

Little nod. "I told her earlier today. She was mad too."

"No shit," I snap. "What were you thinking, Kyra?"

Her chin juts up, her glare boring into me, her voice quiet. "I was thinking that I wanted to spare her the pain I felt when you left. I was thinking I'd spare her the disappointment, the bitterness."

"You can't make everything about that," I argue, storming over to her. "You can't use that to justify everything. Are you really trying to justify this?"

Kyra's glare sags, then she turns away. "I don't know. No, you know - it wasn't right. Not telling you. I know it wasn't. I've wanted to tell you for weeks, over a month now. Even before, part of me thought..." Inhale. Exhale. "But do you know what? I thought of Pamela, and how sad she was when her dad finally came back into her life. How horribly sad she was, with how he'd miss their dinners, drop off the face of the Earth for months at a time. I was just trying to protect Madison, make sure she didn't have to go through that too. I'm sorry, but that's how it was."

Her words are peeling away my rage. They make sense. Too much sense.

But I don't want fucking sense right now. I just want some clarity.

"I'm going to want to see her," I say, half-angrily, half-wearily.

Jesus, I have a daughter.

Kyra nods. "I know. It's probably for the best."

I frown at her. "Damn straight it is."

I swallow, make for the front door.

My hand on the cool silver handle, I pause. "You know, Kyra, what I did was wrong, horrible. But this was pretty fucking terrible too."

"I know," she says softly. "After this, do you think... we can..."

"I don't know," I say. Don't you glance at her. Not a fucking glance. "This... well, this is big. Way bigger than anything I can get my head around right now. I'm not sure I can trust you anymore. Or ever again."

She says nothing, because there is nothing to say to that.

"Night, Kyra," I say, walking out into it.

I get into my Porsche and drive home. The roads are empty, the lights are green and I drive as fast as my foot will dig into the gas pedal.

A kid... I have a kid. Jesus.

A kid. A daughter. An actually cool kid.

And Kyra... how could she not tell me for so fucking long? Especially after we started seeing each other again.

Back at home, whatever's left in the fridge - mainly from Nolan stopping in - I eat. Leftover pizza, cookies, a lonely-looking stalk of celery.

Jesus, a daughter...

My phone rings.

"Hey loser," Nolan says.

"Don't invite girls over to my place when I'm not here," I growl.

Nolan groans. "You really are whipped."

"It's plain common sense," I argue. "A girl like that could be a klepto, a psycho, suicidal..."

"All things I vetted her for, thank you very much," Nolan says with a sniff. "Most guys would be thankful for a hot swimsuit model waiting half-naked on their couch."

"Yeah, well, I'm not. I've had a hell of a weekend, as you know."

"You going to take the deal?"

"Doesn't seem like we have any choice. Anyway, it is a good deal."

"Yeah," Nolan admits, crunching something that's probably chips, "it is."

"That why you're calling me?" I grumble. "To go over what we know already?"

"Nah, I... what's up with you? Disney Weekend that much of a bust?"

"So that's why you're calling?" I growl. "Goodbye, Nolan."

"You pissed because of the model or because I'm right?"

"I'm pissed because I just found out that I'm a father," I snap before I can stop myself.

Fuck.

"Wait - what?" Nolan laughs.

"It's not a joke. Kyra's kid - she's mine."

Even saying it aloud, it doesn't feel real.

"No way," Nolan gasps in a horrified voice. "That's impossible. You get a paternity test?"

"Just a day with her is a paternity test," I grumble back. "I'll send you a pic."

"So, wait - that means I'm an uncle? I now have a decent excuse to go to Fun Haven and pick up hot, lonely single moms?"

"Yeah, not happening."

More crunching. "You're no fun."

More crunching. "And Kyra never told you about this kid?"

"Says I was a kid-hater, and I did dump her pretty shittily."

"Both true," Nolan chimes in.

"Fuck off," I growl.

"Don't shoot the messenger. Still. A kid." Low whistle.

"I know."

"And Kyra?" he continues.

"What about her?"

"You good with her?"

"No, of course I'm not fucking 'good' with her. She didn't tell me about a kid I've had for nine years. Even recently, when we've been seeing each other, she didn't mention it."

"That's fucked," Nolan says, catching on. "What are you going to do?"

When I don't respond, he presses, "Want to know what I think you should do?"

"Nope," I say immediately.

"Forget about her," he says, hastily adding, "Kyra, not the kid. Do your duty by her, visit her or whatever. But as for Kyra? Things are too fucking complicated with that woman. You know I'm right."

When I still don't answer, he says, "Right, well, I'll leave you to it."

'Leaving me to it' only makes me search for more food in my fridge unsuccessfully. And then call her up.

Only she's beat me to it.

"Hey," she says.

"Hey," I say.

"I was just thinking... what if you came back over?" she says. "I know that before... just. There's something I want to say to you in person."

"Not in the mood, Kyra."

"Oh."

"And I won't be for a while. Say it to me here."

Movement on the other end. Sounds like she's walking, or changing the hand that's holding the phone or something.

"Kyra," I say again, "Say it to me here."

"No."

"Do it."

"Landon."

"I want to hear you say it." I already know what she's going to say. I could see this one from a mile off. I'm just so fucking tired, that for once, I'm ready for it. Bring it fucking on.

"This... us... I - "

"Don't think it can work," I finish for her.

"Yeah," she says, voice relieved and sad and something else. "Not now, maybe not ever. I'm sorry."

"Don't be."

"OK, well..." she trails off.

"You'll let me see Madison, though. We can start with a weekend here and there, then see how it goes?" I find myself saying. I had no clue I was going to say that until I did. "I want to be in her life, Kyra."

"Of course," she says. "Good."

"Great," I say.

"Great," she says.

"I should get going," I say.

"Goodbye," she says.

"Goodbye," I say.

And then I hang up the phone.

Only then does it occur to me what I should've said.

CHAPTER 26

Kyra

"So, it's really over then?" Pompom asks, sprawled on the couch beside me. Her wide green eyes over the rim of the Chocolatey Chai tea she's drinking manage to look sympathetic and shocked all at once.

"I think so," I say.

It feels odd, saying it. Not right. Not wrong either, though.

"I don't think it's sunk in yet," I confess. "After all, it's only been a few days."

A few days of radio silence. The weekend's approaching, so I'll probably hear from him then about seeing Madison. Maddy hasn't shut up about it since I told her.

I check the time, but it's still early. The annual review at my work is happening later today.

Then there's this whole reunion with Pompom, which is going well... so far.

She nods, a stray red hair bouncing along with her. "Remember when that ska band guy dumped me it took me, like, months before I cried? And then I couldn't stop crying."

I snort. "Thanks for the vote of confidence."

"Not that you'll do that," Pamela clarifies with a winning smile and eyebrow raise. "You're way stronger than me, remember?"

I roll my eyes and sip my own peppermint tea from the new llama mug she just bought me. "OK, you're laying it on a little thick, there."

She shakes her head stubbornly. "Nope. Nothing short of me getting on hands and knees is too much. I'm just glad you agreed to see me at all."

"I'm still not even mostly over it," I confess.

"I know." Pamela bites her lip. "It's only been days. I was a bit surprised you agreed to see me this morning."

"Me too," I say with a shrug. "Maybe it's the whole Landon thing. Maybe my brain can only handle being mad at a limited number of people at once."

She sets her empty mug on the side glass coffee table. "You're mad at him?"

"Maybe." I shrug again. "Maybe a bit. I guess I thought that, after everything, he would fight for us. No matter what. He kept coming back, kept trying to make things work. Then again, I did betray his trust hugely. And I'm not sure I even want him to try to make this work. I think we need to just let it go."

Pamela reaches over to squeeze my hand. "I don't know. I'm not as sure as you are that things are over over. How do you know that when he shows up to pick up Madison, the romantic music in the back of your heads won't start playing... and your eyes won't meet... and..."

"I don't know," I admit with a shrug. "It just feels over now." I set my mug down with a sigh. Time for a change of subject. "I'm pretty sure I'm going to lose my job today."

"I swear," Pamela says, reaching over to squeeze my other hand. "Once my old bestie from high school comes through, you've got first dibs on a job, before me."

"I appreciate it," I say with a smile. "Though I have zero experience in graphic design - unless you count those epic cover pages for our book reports back in primary."

Pamela laughs so hard that a little snort comes out. "Oh my God, you and your Comic Sans. Plus, that rainbow background you couldn't seem to get enough of."

"It was a hella pretty rainbow background, I'll have you know," I say stiffly, although a giggle is traveling up my throat.

In the end, Pamela stays with me right until it's time to go for my meeting. She even comes along for the ride there.

"I've got things to do in the city," she says offhand, which may or may not be true. "Anyway, you need the moral support. Even though you're going to totally ace it."

"It might not be up to me," I say, trying not to let my nerves show.

If I let what's working away at me out, then I might just not be able to put it away again.

The roads are annoyingly empty and every light's a green, as if they're all mockingly egging me on towards my doom.

I drop Pamela off before going to park. Then, I walk inside.

Jackson and Peterson. New York's top law firm. Maybe my former employer. Not if I have anything to say about it.

The building is an old train station, with its original facade, all curving arches and a bit of ambitious taupe brickwork. Walking inside, I'm reminded of why I fell in love with the place. Brimming and bustling with productive, talented people doing productive, talented things, it breathes efficiency.

Not like that student government job I had back in college where every other employee had a tab open to Facebook for the seven hours a day they did little to no work, no. Here, productivity is a way of life.

Even the receptionist is busy, four calls on hold while she talks to the fifth, nodding to me to go in.

This is it. Today's the day.

The day when everything could change.

Last time I came in here nervous and uncertain was for my interview. Everyone looked older, more sure of themselves than I felt. Part of me vibrated with a certainty that they'd laugh me out of here, top law school student or no.

Of course, they didn't. I impressed them, charmed them, and they hired me on the spot.

And I haven't let them down. Until now.

As a lawyer, there are some things you just don't do. Unspoken rules that you don't break.

Sleeping with the opposition is one of them.

Inside the conference room, someone's cranked up the AC. Goose bumps pebble along my arms inside of my stuffy blazer. Another day for my Hugo suit - the best one I own - and I still feel like a murderer being walked to the noose.

The faces in the room I all recognize, just as I recognize the looks on their faces: unfriendly, condemning. Or maybe I'm just scared shitless.

Kara is the other top lawyer. Her silky black hair is scalped back into a severe ponytail, her red-lipped mouth clearly trying not to show satisfaction that she's all set to be on top. Paul and his pasty white hands are folded with an unctuous expression. He tried to hit on me once and I turned him down. And then there's Terence. Silver hair, blank expression, crystalline blue eyes. The boss. Kingpin. The guy I usually get kindly, fatherly vibes from, even though in the courtroom he's nothing short of a maverick.

Now, I'm definitely not getting fatherly vibes from him.

"First things first," he says briskly, frowning at me. "Kyra, you're fired. You know why."

"We won the case," I argue. "What else matters?"

"What else matters?" Terence laughs harshly, bowing his silver head to shoot me a beady look. "What matters is that I can't trust you or your judgment anymore. You stalled on the Storm case, didn't realize you had the main witness right under your nose... No. I don't make the same mistake twice."

"We would've won the case anyway," I point out, "and I've never let my personal life get in the way of my professional duties before."

"Paying lip service to what you should've done isn't going to win me over," Terence continues, eyes narrowed. "We both know you screwed up."

"I screwed up," I agree. "No denying it. But I don't make the same mistake twice either. Give me another chance."

"No," he says. "You went too far this time. Sleeping with the opposition? This isn't some fucking romcom."

"Terence," I begin.

The creak of the door opening. I swing around.

Him.

"This not a good time?" Landon says, pausing uneasily.

"It's a great time," I say smoothly, "I was just getting fired."

"Well," he says, "in that case... I wanted to tell you that I realized something these past few days."

I gape at him. Where the heck is this going? And why is my heart doing the Macarena?

"Can this wait?" Terence asks icily. "We're in a meeting now, Mr. Storm."

"No," Landon says. "No, it really can't."

Everyone's watching. Oh God. What could be so important that he had to come here to say it?

Landon turns to me. "I love you," he says simply, "And I don't want to live without you. I don't care what it takes. I don't care what I have to do. I want to be with you."

Terence scowls. "Is this really the - "

"Shut up," Landon says, not even looking at him. He only has eyes for me.

"Kyra," he says, "you don't have to answer me now. But I needed to tell you that. Needed you to know that."

I gawk at him. I probably look like a complete mouth-agape, eyes-bugged kook, but I can't help it.

After what he said before, what we decided, I thought...

He walks up to me, grasping both my hands. I rise. We eye each other. Everyone else, everything else, fades away.

Except for that goddamn overeager air conditioner.

"Will you do this with me?" he says.

Will I? He's wearing that pink shirt, and I want to laugh, to cry. I've just lost a job, but I've gained a man.

The answer is obvious.

"Yes," I say. "Hell yes."

CHAPTER 27

Kyra

6 months later

"Phew, she's finally in bed," Landon says, ambling into the bedroom with a tired yet happy smile. "Thought she'd get me to read Babar a third time."

"You're such a sucker for her," I tease him, not looking up from my book. I'm almost done with the chapter, and Kate Morton isn't letting me leave any sooner.

And yet... Landon draws my gaze like a bee to honey. I'm going to have to tell him tonight. I've only known a day, but he'll kill me if I keep it from him any longer.

"What can I say?" Landon's smile is relaxed, easy. He's been smiling like that a whole lot lately. "I love my daughter."

I grin.

Madison loves him too. Adores him, is the word. They're two peas in a pod, those two. Both love biking, Indiana Jones - and not replacing the toilet roll once it's finished, but we're working on that one.

"So, what do you say?" Landon says, coming over to sit beside me, turning my face to his. "First night in our new house... first time?"

I put the book aside. "Oh?"

Next second, he's climbing onto the bed, his body pressing into mine.

"Did I ever mention I love you?" he asks, as our lips lock and relock.

I pull away to giggle. "Only every day."

"Good," he says, lips back on mine.

His hands run through my hair, and our pelvises move together to a beat only we can hear.

"Alexa, some Diana Krall," Landon says, and next second she's crooning along to the flow of our bodies.

"You Casanova, you," I tease through the kisses.

"Nothing's too good for my girl," he says, smiling down at me. "Now, less talking, more kissing."

He doesn't have to ask me twice. He tastes like the ribs he barbecued us for dinner in the background - and a bit of the Ben and Jerry's mint ice cream Maddy begged us to have after.

His hands run along my body, under my clothes, sending tremors of pleasure in their wake.

We've been making love for months - in every position and every way, most nights and some days - and it never gets old.

Not with the skillful stroke of his hands, how he knows how to get me groaning in seconds. How his mouth and hands seem to know me better than I know myself.

Just like now.

His hands caress my breasts as his fingers press into my clit. His fingertips swirl around my nipple, tweaking them.

Just like that, it comes on me all at once: the peaking, the groaning, the orgasm.

But Landon's just getting started. He fingers me and caresses my breasts and ass and body, and then he eats me out until I've come so many times I've lost track.

Jesus, the man can't seem to get enough of my body.

Not that I'm anywhere near getting enough of his.

His lips sweep down, fastening on a nipple, then his fingers sweep inside me.

"So wet," he growls, pleased.

My hands go under his pants to his cock.

"So hard," I moan.

I stroke his erection with one hand, while the other works on his belt. Off go his pants, his briefs.

Then, I clamber on top of him.

"Oooh yeah," I groan, lowering myself onto him.

Already, I'm close. Just the perfect fit of him inside me is enough to bring me to the edge.

Mmmmm...

I grind my hips back and forth, throwing myself up and down. His hands go to my ass and enjoy the flesh there. He massages it like it's some kind of meditation. It feels amazing, the rhythm of our bodies moving together so slowly, almost unbearably slowly, with so much pleasure at the edge that I'm not sure I can take it.

Until, out of nowhere, a spank - and my orgasm slams through me. I sink onto him, trembling all over, while he takes a nipple in his mouth.

Fucking yes...

Another spank - and another orgasm.

Another - and another.

Afterwards, he turns me around so that I'm on all fours, brain woozy with pleasure. Then he fucks me like mad, our bodies slapping together.

"I"

Slap

"Fucking"

Slap

"Love"

Slap

"You!" he exclaims.

And then, clasping each other, trembling, we come together.

As we lie there, once our breathing has slowed, I can't help peering at him with a dopey smile.

"What?" he says, smiling like a handsome dope himself.

"I just can't believe... that this is our life," I murmur, leaning in to give him a kiss. And another. "That it's all worked out."

"What - that we have a house in Hyde Park with our amazing daughter who's top in her class?" Landon asks, grin growing as he speaks, "That we get to work together? That Storm Inc. is doing better than ever? That you've gone solo as a lawyer and are killing it?"

"Among a few things," I admit with a giggle.

"That's not all, though," he says, face finally going somber.

"What do you mean?" I ask.

He throws me a sidelong look. "I think you'll need a robe first."

"For?"

His eyebrows leap. "Can't tell you yet."

My smile goes sassy. "And if I refuse?"

Next second, he's tickling my armpit and I'm busting out with dismayed giggles. "Fine, fine - OK!"

Once I've got on the teal oriental robe he bought me on our trip to Japan, and he's got on his robe too, he takes me by the arm.

"Do I get to find out where you're taking me?" I ask with an amused smile.

He looks half-amused, half-intense. What could it be? "Not yet."

He leads me down the stairs, over to the back door. Over the deck and...

Holy... shit.

This is not the backyard I saw only hours ago when we were directing the movers where to put our stuff and later, when he barbecued our first meal as a family at our new home. No, now, lit up by strings of lights, its thousand square feet is filled with rose petals.

I wheel around to gape at Landon. "Landon... what? When did you have time to do this?"

"Nolan owed me one," he explains with a grin, getting down on one knee.

He gets out a tiny felt box, and all I can seem to do is gape at him.

What the actual hell? This can't be happening, can it?

"Kyra," he says.

"Landon," I say.

Part of me is expecting to wake up. Isn't this another one of those shimmering bubbles destined to be popped?

"I've wanted to do this since the second month I knew you," Landon's saying, voice low, gaze steady on me. "I've had this ring since college. That was part of what made me freak out and ruin everything, knowing that I was so young and so sure of you that I bought a fucking ring." He grimaces, gives his head a little shake as he opens the lid. "But I made the mistake of losing you once - there's no way in hell I'll be doing that again. I want to spend the rest of my life with you."

Inside is a gorgeous ring - carved silver hearts with a diamond surrounded by rubies, my birthstone, the one I always loved when I was younger. He remembered. He did this. He's doing this.

This isn't a fragile bubble - this is as real as the daughter we share together.

"Kyra," he says, "will you be my wife?"

Whoa.

Holy...

Whoa.

A startled giggle falls out of me.

And yet Landon's face is tensed, expectant... oh yeah, expecting a response, you dummy.

"Yes," I blurt out. "God, yes!"

We embrace.

"There's something I have to tell you too," I say as we separate.

"Something that can top this?" he jokes, as he slides the ring onto my finger.

Perfect fit. Even in the somber light, it's gorgeous.

"I'll leave that for you to decide," I reply, patting my belly.

The smile on Landon's face as his eyes light up is so sweet it's almost heartbreaking. "No."

I'm grinning myself as I pat my belly again. "Yes. Madison's going to have a little sister."

Landon kneels to give my belly a kiss. "Two little girls. Aren't I the luckiest man alive." He rises to give me a kiss. "I love you."

"And I love you." I kiss him back.

And all I can seem to think is: what's better than being married to the love of your life?

Raising a family with him.

~*The End*~

If you LOVED Enemy's Secret, be sure to check out Just Pretend!

It's a fun and flirty hot romance read filled with page melting heat, lots of teasing, drama and some sugar sweet moments guaranteed to leave you with a very satisfying happily-ever-after.

https://www.ashleepriceromanceauthor.com/ **or direct**

https://www.ashleepriceromanceauthor.com/product/just-pretend-an-accidental-text-fake-engagement-romance-love-comes-to-town-book-3/

JUST PRETEND SNEAK PEEK

Here's the deal.

I'll be your unexpected hero.

You can be my fake fiancé.

And...we've got 90 days to figure everything out.

Nolan

I knew she was trouble when she showed up with my phone.

The sway of those hips.

The smile on her lips when I say something funny.

Sweet with just the right amount of sass.

You're not supposed to fall in love with the woman you randomly bump into at the bar.

And she's not supposed to accidentally text you something NSFW.

But here we are.

Drawn together like magnets.

I knew this could end in heartbreak.

But I'll stop at nothing to make her mine past the 90 days.

Even if we lose everything.

Including each other.

Sierra

He's my polar opposite. Mr. Grump.

The wealthy black sheep brother from the infamous Storm family.

I wasn't supposed to go through his phone.

But one accidental text later, I can't seem to quit him.

What's a girl to do when a gorgeous rich guy bumps into you?

Well, you could tell him where to go.

You could also tell the clumsy jerk that he dropped his phone.

Or, you could secretly unlock it,

To discover photos and texts that'll make you blush.

And when he unexpectedly texts back,

Make sure you don't forget to follow the unwritten rules of texting.

Be unique. Tease him.

Leave him wanting more.

And...marry him in 90 days?!

https://www.ashleepriceromanceauthor.com/

or direct

https://www.ashleepriceromanceauthor.com/product/just-pretend-an-accidental-text-fake-engagement-romance-love-comes-to-town-book-3/

Chapter 1

Nolan

"You have to be married in three months," Emerson blurts out.

I stare at him.

Married... three months...

The words don't seem to go together.

Emerson is still tracing that infinity symbol into the chocolate cake remnants on his plate, but there's almost no chocolate left. His stainless-steel fork is scraping across one of the porcelain plates we got a deal on from some supplier that was going out of business and remembered a favor Dad did for them once upon a time. But the main thing is that what he just said, that crazy talk, was out-of-fucking-bounds and im-fucking-possible.

Dad wouldn't have put in such a useless, out-of-left-field requirement. He just wouldn't.

His voice echoes in my head: "Don't end up like me, Nolan boy, old, sad, alone and regretful. You find yourself a good girl, you stick with her, no matter what. Even when it's hard."

I scowl, even though it's my own dumb-ass brain bringing back these blasts from the past.

C'mon, that was one late night in some weird underground speakeasy when Dad was drunk on this terrible wine from Greenland, of all places, and had just found out that Mom had remarried.

"Nolan?" Landon prompts.

I can feel his gaze nudging me to look at him. But I can hear the sympathy in his voice, and I don't want to see it in his face. I don't want his fucking sympathy.

Kyra and Harley just look sad, like I'm a puppy dog who got kicked, who they might give a hug if I so much as sniffle. Although a hug is the last thing I need right now.

Whatever Emerson—the most honest brother of all of us—said, it can't be true.

"You can't be serious," I say lightly.

To think I actually bought it for a second there. I guess I had this coming, though; with all the pranks and jokes I've pulled on my brothers over the years—Landon's still pissed about those shrimp tails I hid in his curtain rod that took him a good two months to find—they were bound to seek retribution sometime.

Although I can't say this is their best work. Out of all the shit they could've claimed Dad specified in his will, there's about a thousand things that I would've bought before this: Dad having about twelve illegitimate children he's leaving money to, Dad having learned he's the son of Putin and wanting us to visit him, a pet polar bear for each of us. But not this. No fucking way.

"You've got to be kidding me," I insist.

But none of them—Greyson, Harley, Emerson, Kyra—will meet my eye. As for Landon... when I finally meet his eye, the expression there is as good as a condemnation.

"No fucking way," I hiss, although this time it's nothing more than sheer denial.

30 minutes earlier...

Sometimes all it takes is a glimpse. For Sierra Hill, it took even less.

Not that I know it yet—I don't have a fucking clue.

Right now, she's just a split-second once-over: hot little Coke-bottle body, brown-red hair the color of that delicious red velvet cake Mom used to make us for our birthdays, blue startled eyes, the curling of a generous lower lip that could be the cousin to a smile.

Yeah, a half-second glimpse that ends with me knowing. Not her name, not yet.

Just that I want what I see.

Too bad now's not a good time. It's a really fucking shitty time, actually.

Tonight's not about me. Although maybe later, once the dinner's over...

Tearing my gaze off her as she continues to the bathroom, I raise my glass and my smile to the others at the table. "Here's to my brother and his love—may you be as happy as you look."

Everyone chuckles, although Landon shoots me a glare.

I just wink. "You almost make being engaged look palatable."

Something's been up with him tonight. Something that's making his responses come seconds too late, his smiles too. Something that he's not saying.

We're at the Miller comedy club and restaurant, although the comedy club is out of commission. It's under renovation—renovations which I'm overseeing, unfortunately. Normally, I like construction and supervising, but this project has been plagued by one mishap after another.

Right now, Landon's bringing the back of Kyra's hand to his lips, affection kindling in his hazel eyes. "What can I say—this girl makes it easy."

She chuckles with a toss of her dark-haired head, before leaning in for a kiss. "You smooth-talker, you."

I glance away, but the woman from before is long gone, of course. Not that it matters much. You catch one, you lose one—was that what Dad used to say after he and Mom called it quits and he embarked on his epic dating spree that culminated in some Victoria's Secret model, and that the rest of us have yet to match?

Not that my other brothers are really trying. Greyson, the eldest, is married and has a kid. Even goddamn Landon, who I had pegged for a forever bachelor like myself after his university love debacle, ended up engaged to said university love debacle—hence the whole reason for this dinner—and with a kid. Emerson is still loyal to the bachelor cause, but who knows for how long, with this new Polish girlfriend—Monica, Molly, Maude—that he won't shut up about.

Landon's started on me too, lately, with the odd suggestion I find my own 'Kyra' here, the Dad-esque comments that I can't be a bachelor forever there. Weird.

Hell, Landon has always been the 'Responsible Twin', but now that he knows he's a father it seems like that's translated into him as the 'Responsibly Annoying Twin'. Jesus. I can't even remember the last time all of us brothers went out on the town together and got shitfaced.

"The place is looking good for being under renovation," Emerson says, with a look around.

I swallow back the urge to point out that this front restaurant area is the only one we'll be keeping open for now, and strictly by necessity. And that once we're finished with it, the yawn-worthy stucco walls and cement parking-garage-esque floor will be replaced by something unrecognizable. Something my overzealous and overpaid designer Melinda assured me would be 'WOW'. She did show me a bunch of pictures of her 'mood board' for the area that didn't make me want to vomit, so we were a go.

"You should see the back," I grumble instead.

"That bad, eh?" he says, all sympathetic connivance.

That's the thing about my little brother, God bless him. He isn't good at pretending he cares—he does one better: he actually cares.

"We're months behind and will probably be months more behind, thanks to fucking Gerard's mishaps," I mutter, eyeing the bar warily.

That asshole spent more time here drinking than he did working, and it came across in his completely fucked measurements for every room. Tool didn't even apologize, either. I finally fired the idiot, but not before his fuck-ups cost us months, at least. Dickwad.

I give my head a little shake. "Anyway, it's good to be here with everyone." I gesture at Landon and Kyra. "And look at those two lovebirds."

"Picked where you'll be heading for the honeymoon?" Emerson asks the happy couple, smiling over the rim of his wineglass at them. I'm pretty sure that's his third glass.

For all his mooning over this M chick, he has started drinking more since he's been seeing her.

"We're just trying to get through the wedding first," Kyra confesses with a happy little laugh.

Landon gives her an even happier kiss. Christ, I know they're in loooove, but how many times can you feel like kissing the same person in a matter of consecutive minutes? "By 'we', she means 'her'. One quick visit with the wedding planner was all it took for us to figure out that I have zero taste."

He says that like hemming and hawing for hours over napkin shapes and doily fabrics is anything other than an elaborate 20th century form of male torture.

"Babe," Kyra says, a smile cracking on her red lips, "you were going to have our color scheme be gray and silver."

"I stand by what I said," Landon states stoutly. "Sensible colors, both of them."

The rest of us chuckle. I try to keep my face lighter than my thoughts: that what Landon's doing is anything but sensible. Yeah, Greyson and Harley make the whole marriage thing look easy, but they've been at it a little over a year. And sure, Landon has been in love with Kyra since forever, but when was that ever a recipe for marital bliss?

What he should be doing is what I'm doing: taking a page out of Mommy and Daddy dearests' marriage handbook and see the whole thing as the losing game it is.

I nudge Greyson and ask him in an undertone, "Chosen a gift yet? I call dibs on that panda onesie for that kid."

"Her name's Madison," he grumbles. "And she's eight. That link you sent me could fit a five-year-old, maybe."

"I know what her name is," I grumble back. "I'm her favorite uncle, remember? And anyway, that's what zippers are for: squeezing into outfits that aren't a perfect fit. Plus, when she gets like, I don't know, sixteen or something, she can donate that beauty of an outfit to Dakota."

"Wonderful," Greyson says, running a hand through his coiffed dark hair.

"Oh stop," Harley says to him, a half-grin showing the gap between her front teeth. Her sandy blonde hair is gathered in two fishtail braids that would look ridiculous on anyone else. "That panda outfit is hilarious." She cranes up her head so that her chin rests on his shoulder with a knowing smile. "Besides, you're just grumpy because…" As his scowl grows, she trails off, moving away with a shake of her head. "Forget it."

"Forget what?" I ask. Tonight is starting to annoy me, and it's not just that someone went all fruity scented candle-happy with our tables in the two hours I left to go home and veg out. "Seems like everyone's in on some bad news I don't know about. Or are you all still pissed that I skipped Dad's will reading? I told you, batty old Aunt Edna has it in for me."

I stifle a shudder. Her and most of Dad's extended family. They being majorly old-fashioned means that one look at my tattooed, long-haired self will send any one of them into a days-long rant about 'kids these day'. Never mind that I'm thirty-fucking-two.

"Oh, speaking of," Emerson chimes in, light blond head bowed as he digs through the leather messenger bag he has slung on his chair. "She wanted me to give you these." He takes out a familiar Barney-purple tin bedecked with gaudy golden lettering and I groan.

"You see? Does she give anyone else eons-expired chocolate mints from the '70s? No, I think not."

The others crack up, although I'm not finished yet. I take the tin and give it a shake, suspiciously eyeing its bottom. Most of the lettering is faded and I can't seem to find a manufacture date, which isn't necessarily a promising sign.

I pause, my suspicious glance moving on to them. Normally, one of them chimes in to defend the old witch—after all, she usually gives them a crisp hundred-dollar bill on every occasion ranging from Halloween to Hanukkah, despite the fact that we aren't Jewish, and she does play a mean game of table tennis.

Hell, something's definitely up.

"OK, no shit," I tell him. "Spill. What's this shitty secret of yours?"

Greyson, Landon and Emerson exchange a look.

"Don't tell me," I grumble. "Dad had some more surprises in his will."

Not that I'm overly worried. Our father-son relationship might have been rocky in my teen years, but it ended up OK. I did go into business at Storm Inc. how he wanted, after all. Sure, it was part-time, and sure, I focused more on my comedy career, but still. Plus, Dad was never stingy with us—just a bit strict, that was all.

Even if in business, he was as slippery as an eel.

All things considered, at the end of the day, he was a good dad, and a shitty human being. If I didn't know any better, I'd think that I missed him.

Who knows, maybe I do. Maybe.

"Now isn't really the time," Greyson is saying carefully, his jaw tensed, gesturing to Landon and Kyra. After all, this dinner is to celebrate them.

"Don't hold back on account of me," Landon says, taking a sip of his water as he eyes the others. "The sooner Nolan knows, the better."

"I don't know...." is all Emerson contributes uncertainly, twiddling his spoon.

I'm about ready to brandish my knife at these doofuses. They know how much I hate being out of the loop, and they pull this?

Instead, I grit my teeth together, place the flat of both palms on the table, and, in a voice so calm motherfucking Buddha would give me props, say, "The sooner Nolan knows what, the better?"

I've had about as much of this as I can take. Yes, it's supposed to be a celebratory dinner for Landon and his perfect relationship with his high school sweetheart, but fuck it, my brothers just need to tell me what's up and get it over with.

"It's Dad's will," Greyson says, his face already sympathetic. "He's leaving everything to us equally—but yours has a condition."

All of a sudden, everyone at the table looks away, as if I have scabby leprosy or some shit.

"Which is?" I say.

I might as well pull this Band-Aid off nice and fast.

But they're all sitting there speechless, as if saying it is as good as starting a countdown to my demise.

Emerson is carving a chocolaty infinity symbol into the remnants of his chocolate mousse cake. Landon's hazel-eyed gaze on me is assessing, as if trying to track my response already. Greyson's sculpted face is blank; he's probably playing footsie under the table with that wife of his. Meanwhile, my brain churns over what it could be. Some kind of stupid ethics course? A forced visit to clean up that island we always suspected he had? He found out about my casino loss all those years ago and is instating a ban?

"Guys," I growl.

"You have to be married in three months," Emerson blurts out.

GET MORE FROM ASHLEE PRICE

Amazon lists millions of titles, and I'm happy you discovered this one.

But if you'd like to know when I release a new book, instead of leaving it up to chance, sign up for my newsletter.

I'll send you an email when my latest release goes live.

https://www.ashleepriceromanceauthor.com/signup/

www.ingramcontent.com/pod-product-compliance
Lightning Source LLC
Chambersburg PA
CBHW060913210726
48293CB00006B/2090